What Mitsy Did Next

Book 3 in the Mitsy Howard trilogy

Also by this author

14 Viney Hill
TravelWorks
HomeWorks
Oh, and another thing…
The Enduring Curiosity of Mitsy Howard: A Walk in the Mill
Mitsy Howard: In the Dark

What Mitsy Did Next

Book 3 in the Mitsy Howard trilogy

Carole Susan Smith

ISBN: 978-1-916820-97-5

PublishNation
www.publishnation.co.uk

*'What Mitsy Did Next' is dedicated to
my friends and neighbours
in the village of Staunton
in the beautiful Forest of Dean,
to thank them for
their kindness and support*

About the Author

The opportunity to do many unusual things and to work in other countries including Siberia, the Palestinian Occupied Territories, the Far East, across Europe as well as in the UK, has provided the source for Carole's light-hearted memoirs.

The inspiration for her novels – *14 Viney Hill, The Enduring Curiosity of Mitsy Howard - A Walk in the Mill, Mitsy Howard in the Dark* and *What Mitsy Did Next* -- has been her overactive imagination.

1

"I'm going to have my colours done tomorrow," said Mitsy to Eva as she ran her fingers through her hair. "How about you?"

Eva looked a little puzzled. "I just had my hair done last week. I think it's OK for now."

Eva was new to Appledore House and so she was unsure how things were organised here but she appreciated Mitsy's kindness in helping her settle in.

"Oh no," said Mitsy. "I meant I'm going to that session that's being held here in the dining room tomorrow afternoon. You know how as you get older your hair changes colour; your skin tone alters and all the clothes you bought when you were younger look wrong and don't fit nicely? Well, there's a 'colour consultant' coming to advise us on our colours. My friend went to a session once and she told her she was autumn colours. That meant that gold, orange and brown shades looked best on her. It was funny really because she ended up sending most of her clothes to the charity shop and buying new. And new make-up. I seem to remember her husband was not best amused!"

Eva smiled, "oh, that sounds like a good idea. I've never had my colours done! Where do we pay?"

"No need. It's all part of the events and entertainment that Appledore House organises for residents. There's a notice on the sideboard in the dining room. You just sign up to say you will go. I think sometimes if they choose something no one signs up for, they cancel it. Of course, there are probably maximum numbers but I've always been able to go to everything I've signed up for."

Eva nodded. She had not really expected anything so pleasant. Before she moved into Appledore House she was rather worried that everyone would sit around dozing all day with a nurse calling in occasionally to make them do exercises. It was turning out much better than she had feared.

"In the summer we have outings too. A minibus takes us to National Trust properties and we even had a riverboat trip on the canal once. Of course, the pandemic put a stop to the outings but things are starting to get better now."

Mitsy had gently steered Eva to the dining room where they found a clipboard leaning up against a china dog. Eva was happy to sign up and to take part. There was a maximum of ten people for tomorrow and only five names listed so far. Mitsy wondered out loud whether it was open to men but they concluded that the men probably didn't need make-up advice!

Currently, Appledore House had seven men and twelve women residents so anything Maggie organised needed to be suitable for the majority as well as not excluding the rest.

Mitsy left Eva at the door to her room, as she was meeting her friend Arthur for lunch today.

During the coronavirus pandemic, Appledore House had been very careful to follow all the guidance set out by the government during its televised announcements. Residents were required to stay in their rooms alone, where meals and medication were delivered by staff wearing personal protective equipment.

One day, one of the residents who was always known to be a bit perverse and difficult, flouted the rules by going out to the post office. Sadly, she caught the virus, rapidly succumbed to covid19 and died soon after. Lucy's death was a shock to many of the residents and brought into sharp focus the real dangers of the virus. Everyone began to accept that the rules were there to protect them.

It was a difficult time for all, not least the staff. A small group of them generously agreed to move in to the care home for the duration (not that anyone knew how long that would be), living in a motorhome and a couple of the unoccupied rooms. Of course, this meant that they were not able to be with their own families for which Mitsy and her fellow residents were much indebted. Eventually, once testing for coronavirus became available and more reliable, the 'skeleton staff' as they were known, were given time off so that other members of staff could take their places and relieve them.

Later, special arrangements were made for friends and family members to see their loved ones but this was only possible by booking in advance and visiting one at a time in a temporary building in the garden. By this means they were totally segregated from residents and had to communicate by gesture and through a glass partition.

Gradually the restrictions were partially lifted but still the residents spent a lot of time alone and the staff continued to wear PPE. Thankfully, when the weather was good, the garden became a favourite place for people to meet, enabling everyone to have some face to face conversation while keeping a social distance.

It will never be known how much the enforced solitude affected people. Many of the residents had been used to living alone before they moved into Appledore House but even they found the lack of human contact difficult to bear.

Before the pandemic, good friends Mitsy and Arthur were in the habit of spending one lunchtime each week in each other's company. They usually went to the nearby Standsfield Arms where they invariably had a ploughman's lunch; Mitsy had a glass of dry white wine and Arthur had a half pint of the local bitter ale. They were well known to the owners and had even held a celebratory meal when their offspring Pete and Jackie got engaged.

Eventually all the residents of Appledore House were told they could go out again, if they wore a face mask when indoors. Mitsy and Arthur were quite amused as they realised that would make having a meal and drink impossible. However, Arthur suggested that they could have a walk along the road to the pub which they considered to be their local, so they could check whether eating and drinking in the pub garden would be possible, avoiding the need for a face covering.

The whole experience felt strange, to be 'out in the world' again. They agreed that the short walk would be good for them but neither felt sufficiently confident to do more than walk there and back the first day. Discussing this with their fellow residents, it seemed that several of the others had felt uncomfortable on their first outing too.

Gradually life returned to what was often called 'the new normal.' "Shall we venture out for a bite to eat on Wednesday?" Arthur asked Mitsy one morning. Mitsy considered this briefly and then nodded.

The meals at Appledore House were good, so that wasn't really the reason the pair went to the pub. It was just that they both felt it stopped them from getting too insular. After a lifetime of self-reliance, moving into a care home could feel quite restrictive for many people.

Mitsy had settled in to Appledore House quite well, relinquishing housework, shopping, cooking, and gardening with pleasure. She soon made friends with the staff and other residents as well as enjoying the occasional visit from her son Pete when he was able to get time out from his work. When Arthur moved in, Mitsy was one of the first to offer the hand of friendship to him. So it was that a weekly pub lunch became their custom.

Going out had become such a strange occurrence that on Wednesday morning Mitsy stood in front of her wardrobe wondering what to wear. It amused her to think that the whole business of lockdowns had meant that many of the residents had started to wear pyjamas, track suits or other casual clothes most days.

She opened the wardrobe and scanned the row of hangers. She had a very smart suit which had not been worn, that she was saving for when Pete and Jackie got married. Next to that was a long-sleeved black and white houndstooth dress that looked quite smart under her black leather jacket. She glanced at the window and concluded that this would probably be safe enough unless the weather changed dramatically.

Not that she would admit it to anyone else, but it seemed she had gained some weight during the pandemic. 'That's not surprising, as I've had no exercise,' she muttered to herself. Mitsy could often be found having silent conversations with herself – it was obvious because her lips were moving - and if anyone ever mentioned it, she would smile and explain that at least she got sensible answers that way.

Meanwhile, upstairs in his own room Arthur was having a similar clothing dilemma. He was always a smartly dressed man and he felt that it was a matter of courtesy to look presentable when he went out. His wife had always chosen his clothes and when she passed away, it took him quite a while to refresh and replace his older clothes without her guidance. As much as anything else, every item he took from his drawers or wardrobe had a story attached. 'Ivy bought this shirt for me before we went on that first holiday to Scotland. It was so cold, that I nearly didn't wear it at all!' he remembered.

He was fond of Mitsy and she had become a good friend since he moved in to Appledore House but he was very aware that no one could replace his Ivy.

As the hall clock chimed twelve, Arthur was pleased to see Mitsy walking down the corridor towards him.

"Ready?" he asked, as if they were setting off on an adventure, which perhaps they were.

They hung up their room keys on the board by the door, showing that rooms six and fourteen were unoccupied. This was mainly for the benefit of the staff who would then be able to clean the vacated rooms. Later in the day, the key board was useful to show if anyone had failed to return after going out. This rarely happened and anyone showing the slightest sign of forgetfulness of this nature was carefully looked after until it became necessary to move them to one of the other homes that specialised in dementia care. Mrs Podsiadlo, the previous matron and owner of Appledore House, was accommodated in a special care home of this type.

"I've told Vicky in the kitchen that we didn't want lunch today," said Arthur.

With that, they closed the heavy door quietly behind them, crossed the large, gravelled, parking area and turned down the road towards the pub.

Since the pandemic, Arthur had become a little less stable on his feet and had taken to using a walking stick. Mitsy had not realised that this modification would change their walking pace and it took her a little while to adjust. Being a thoughtful and considerate person, she managed to appear to amble slowly alongside Arthur without drawing attention to this.

The Standsfield was barely a ten minute walk away and when they arrived Arthur put his head round the door to ask if they could eat in the pub garden. It seemed that was no problem at all and they walked round the side of the building to where some tables were set out.

One of the young women servers appeared immediately to ask what they would like to eat and drink.

"Oh, I think we will have a glass of dry white wine and half of bitter, for old times' sake," said Arthur, glancing at Mitsy to check that she agreed.

"Have you been here before, then?" asked the young woman. Mitsy was all too happy to recount the many times she and Arthur had enjoyed their Wednesday lunches.

"That's nice. I'm quite new here. I lost my last job because of covid but I was lucky to get this job straight away when they had a vacancy here," she chatted. Within minutes the owner of the pub came out to greet them, carrying their drinks. She was keen to find out how they had been, as well as sharing news of how the pub had fared during the pandemic. Apparently, the Standsfield Arms had struggled quite badly during the lockdowns and they had to make virtually all the staff redundant. She intimated that they were only just getting things back to normal.

"Now, we have a new menu. Did Louise tell you?"

Arthur and Mitsy shook their heads in unison. "I'll get her to bring you one."

"We haven't said hello to Peter yet," said Mitsy.

Peter was the friendly black Labrador that used to sit at their feet every time they visited.

"Oh dear. I'm afraid that's another piece of sad news you have missed. Peter was taken ill right at the beginning of the pandemic. We couldn't take him to the vet as they hadn't sorted out their covid arrangements and by the time we did take him he was too poorly to be helped. I'm sorry but we had to have him put to sleep."

Mitsy blinked and blew her nose loudly and Arthur shook his head. They had both become fond of the dog.

"We do have a new puppy though and I will bring him to see you later."

Smiling, she went back into the bar and they could hear some orders being taken before Louise came out with the new menu.

"Hmm. I'm not sure what to have," said Arthur.

Mitsy perused the new menu too. "I wish things didn't change. We used to like our ploughman's lunches but now I'm not sure what to choose either."

Eventually they both plumped for toasted cheese sandwiches with a shared side salad. It was tasty and they agreed that the new menu was probably an improvement.

Just as they were getting ready to leave, a small bundle of black fur came rushing into the garden, rapidly followed by Louise. "Mickey, you naughty boy, come here at once!"

This was indeed the new puppy. Inevitably he brought a smile to Mitsy and Arthur's faces and they both concluded that Mickey would be a happy addition to the Standsfield Arms.

Strolling back to Appledore House, they agreed that it had been pleasant to go back to the Standsfield, even though so much had changed.

"I can't believe almost three years have passed. I suppose we are fortunate that although so many people were very ill with covid, not to mention those who died, we two have escaped relatively unscathed," said Arthur.

"I imagine it will be many years before we know the impact of the pandemic on the economy, on missed education, how to deal with long covid and mental health problems," replied Mitsy.

Arthur nodded and smiled. "See you later, Mitsy. Thank you for coming out today."

2

Colours

Julie, the colour consultant, introduced herself as she glanced around the room at the residents who had arrived for the style and colour consultation.

Mitsy was sitting in the front row, looking smartly dressed, with Eva, the new resident next to her.

The other four people sitting behind looked much the same age and so Julie was not surprised to see a mix of white and grey hair, along with one younger woman with long dark hair tied up in a modern bun. The latter was Maggie who ran the care home. She had decided to give herself the afternoon off in order to take part in the session.

Julie began by asking some questions, such as "what are your favourite colours?" and "who can guess what are the current on-trend colours?" She then explained how choice of colour can affect mood, self-confidence, and perception.

The talk moved on to explain that skin tone can alter from one season to the next, as well as when we grow older. This means that make-up we loved when we were in our twenties and thirties may no longer suit our colour palette.

Julie asked for a volunteer and Eva raised her hand to do so. The next part of the session involved materials of various colours being held up to Eva's face while other members of the group voted for their preference. Eventually, Julie revealed which colours had been popular (she said "worked for you") and indicated that the gentle pinks, blues, and lilac colours were summer colours that could be worn as pale and delicate or bold and bright, as long as they remained within the same colour range.

There was some discussion about neutrals and again Julie gave the group guidance on wearing black, navy, brown, burgundy, or grey as well as whites, creams, and pastels. The colours chosen for Eva were divided into her key colours and support colours.

It was all getting very interesting when the tea trolley arrived and they stopped for tea and cake, as well as informal chatter about what they had learned so far.

After the tea break, Julie began by showing – using herself as a model – how clothes in different shapes and styles could enhance or ruin one's appearance. She suggested that she could come back for a further session on shape and style, referencing the TV programme that most of the group had seen with Gok Wan, the image consultant. She did promise not to make them expose themselves to family and friends while naked!

Then, everyone in the group was asked to find a partner so that they could help each other select the most suitable colours while Julie walked round offering suggestions and advice. Mitsy and Maggie worked together and found the whole exercise fun as well as instructive.

The last part of the session was much as Mitsy had expected. They were advised to go through their wardrobe selecting things that were in the wrong colour or those that had not been worn for a year. The latter raised some murmurs of dissent, given that everyone had been in lockdown and unable to wear many of their favourite or 'best' clothes. Julie accepted this and said perhaps it would be best to discard things that had not been worn for four or more years.

To finish, everyone was given a little chart with their own selected season's colours and advice about matching hair colour, make up, jewellery and glasses.

Mitsy was intrigued to find that she was summer too, although her range of colours was more extensive than Eva's.

Eva, no doubt prompted privately by Maggie, gave a little speech to thank Julie for her time, patience, and helpful insights. Everyone applauded and Julie collected her materials and props for the session before leaving with the promise to come back soon.

Back in room six, Mitsy opened her wardrobe and sighed. It looked as though the charity shop would be the recipient of a considerable bundle of lightly worn clothes. On the positive side, her new outfit which had been bought for the impending family wedding, whenever it happened, turned out to reflect her newly established colour palette. "Well, that's a relief," she said to herself.

3

Norma

One morning, after Mitsy had been to the local post office to restock her collection of birthday, condolence, and congratulations cards, she was intrigued to find a young man standing just inside the front door of the house. He was peering closely at one of the oil paintings in the hallway and appeared to be making notes on a clipboard.

Mitsy, ever curious – some might even say nosey – paused to ascertain what was going on. "Hello," she said, "you seem to be looking for something. Can I help?"

The young man straightened up quickly. "Er. No. No thank you," he replied. Bending down he handed Mitsy an envelope. She realised immediately that she had dropped one of her recently purchased greeting cards as she balanced her handbag on the hall table while reaching for her door key.

"Oh, thank you so much. I've only just bought these at the Post Office as I like to have spare cards in just in case there's an unexpected birthday, or death…."

Realising that she was chattering to this stranger unnecessarily, she turned swiftly towards the main corridor and headed towards her room. Room six was warm and comfortable and she sat down immediately, loosening her shoes that were beginning to pinch a bit. She thought no more of her encounter with the young man as she checked her phone for messages. Just as Mitsy was wondering what to do next, there was a gentle knock at her door. It was Kate who lived upstairs.

Kate was a good friend and they had already had shared some adventures.

"Are you OK?" she asked solicitously

"Yes. I'm fine. Shouldn't I be?" she quipped

Kate looked carefully at Mitsy as she sat down on the comfortable old armchair that Mitsy had pointed to.

"Where have you been, Mitsy?" said Kate, with just a trace of concern or possibly irritation.

"Nowhere," replied Mitsy rapidly, almost as if she was guilty of something.

Kate sighed and looked as if she was going to cry, so Mitsy changed her demeanour immediately.

"Why? What's wrong?"

"Well, you know Norma next door has not been very well?"

Mitsy nodded.

"Er. Um. She was much worse this morning. They called an ambulance but sadly she passed away before they could take her to hospital"

Mitsy's eyes filled with tears and the two women hugged each other. They were, sadly, used to fellow residents being taken ill and from time to time this did not end well. Norma was well liked by them both. She had been happy to make her home at Appledore House, having moved from South Africa to be nearer her daughter.

"Oh. I'm so sorry. It's been nice having Norma in number five and she had settled in so well. Does Raymond know?" Raymond, who lived in the room opposite Mitsy, was a quiet and thoughtful man who was fond of all his nearby neighbours.

"I'm afraid it was Raymond who heard Norma calling out and he alerted the staff that they were needed," said Kate.

"Oh dear. I know it comes to all of us sooner or later but this is really quite a shock. I've just been down to the post office to buy some stamps and cards so I wasn't aware that Norma was taken ill."

The two friends sat quietly contemplating the sad news.

"I popped round just to make sure you were OK," said Kate. "I'll leave you in peace for now. Shall I knock for you when it's lunchtime?"

Mitsy nodded as she opened the door for her friend.

After Kate had gone, Mitsy felt at a loss to know what to do. She wasn't in the mood for anything cheerful now. Eventually she checked her emails again and then her bank account, neither of which raised her spirits. Glancing at the clock, she realised that she had roughly an hour before lunch, so she pulled on a jacket in order to go for a quiet walk around the garden.

She was really pleased to see Puss. This was Mitsy's name for a beautiful, shiny black cat that frequented the garden. She called the cat Puss as that was the name of all the cats Mitsy had previously owned. 'Not that anyone owns a cat,' she said to herself. People thought that Puss lived nearby, maybe in one of the new flats and came over the road to enjoy the garden and the attention the residents gave her. Of course, they did worry about Puss crossing the road but no one really knew what to do as the collar she wore did not have any form of identification.

Much later, after a couple of slow circuits of the garden, Mitsy felt a bit better after some deep breathing and quiet contemplation on the loss of Norma her neighbour. Back in her room, the phone rang and it was Kate. "Sorry Mitsy, I washed my hair and it isn't dry yet so I shall be a bit late for lunch. Would you go ahead without me and save me a seat please?"

Mitsy reassured her friend that she would make sure she didn't miss anything tasty. Meals at Appledore House had always been enjoyable and quite a source of daily pleasure for the residents. However, Mitsy was not alone in noticing that the quality and possibly even the quantity of their food had gradually deteriorated and reduced over the last couple of years. Mitsy's son Pete had explained that certain food shortages had occurred for several reasons. The war in Ukraine had led directly to oil and grain no longer being available for export. For the UK, leaving the European Union had also meant that trade with many of the 27 member states had stopped or had become more expensive. Other reasons had been suggested by the government or the news media but as Pete worked for the European Commission, Mitsy was inclined to believe his version of events.

To be honest, they had not really noticed the lack of tomatoes, salad leaf and cucumber during the winter months and although the catering team at the care home had done their best, the more observant amongst the residents had realised that the quality of meat, fruit and vegetables had continued to deteriorate for some time. Unlike many of those people who now needed to use food banks, the residents were somewhat cushioned from the harsher realities of life.

Mitsy walked slowly along the corridor to the dining room. As she turned the corner, she saw a young woman that she did not recognise who was looking at a vase. She turned it upside down, squinted at the manufacturers mark and made a hasty note on her clip board. Turning to another item on the sideboard, she picked it up and proceeded to scrutinise that in much the same way.

Misty couldn't help noticing the blonde hair (probably out of a bottle she said to herself), the copious make up, the plumped-up lips and a tiny butterfly tattoo on the neck.

"Oh, hello," said Mitsy. "Have you lost something?" she realised as soon as she said it that her question sounded a bit foolish.

"Ha-ha, no thank you," she said, "I was just admiring this Clarice Cliff vase, it's lovely, isn't it?" with that, she smiled and headed straight for the door, brooking no further discussion.

'How strange' said Mitsy to herself. 'I wonder what that is all about? Maybe she's a rather nosey relative of one of our residents. Or maybe she's connected with the young man who was looking at the painting in the hall.'

The sound of lively chatter preceded the arrival of three residents and within minutes they were quizzing Mitsy about the demise of her neighbour Norma.

Mitsy was still feeling too upset to talk about it and sensibly, once the little group realised this, the conversation turned to the pleasantly mild weather and what they were likely to be served for lunch.

Kate appeared only a few minutes later and Mitsy was pleased that they could both sit down as the staff came in to set the table.

One of the things that Mitsy had appreciated from the outset at Appledore House was the way all the staff took care to support those with mobility or other problems. It was no surprise that several people had difficulty hearing and others needed a walking stick or a rollator walking aid. Very discreetly, once Mitsy had chosen her place at the table, Tracey – a new member of staff – placed a small set of cutlery beside her. Smaller knives and forks made it much easier for Mitsy to control what she liked to call 'my badly behaved hands.' She was not alone in suffering from rheumatic joints but this modest concession was especially helpful for her.

"So, what can we expect for lunch today, Tracey?" asked one of the older gentlemen.

"Oh. I don't know, Sadiq. I have only just come in. I'm sure the others will have made something tasty," she replied.

At that moment Mitsy's friend Arthur arrived and sat down next to Kate. "How are you both?" he asked quietly, realising that they would both be all too aware of the sad news.

Mitsy nodded and smiled gratefully, knowing that Arthur was sensitive enough not to ask further questions.

As the tables began to fill up with hungry residents, Tracey returned with a tray laden with soup bowls, spoons and – from the delicious smell preceding her – freshly baked bread rolls. "Hooray!" exclaimed one lady when she subsequently carried in a large soup tureen and smilingly served everyone with home made vegetable soup. Suddenly the gentle murmur of conversation was replaced by the sound of crunching bread rolls, the spreading of butter and the clink of spoons against china.

Once everyone had finished, there was a short discussion about which vegetables had been used and a few conversations about plans for the afternoon, then everyone dispersed to their own rooms.

It was only as Mitsy got back to her room that she realised she had not seen Raymond at lunch. She tapped gently at his door and when Raymond opened it, she could see he had been crying.

"Raymond. You missed soup for lunch. Is there anything I can get you?" she asked.

"No. I'm fine thank you Mitsy. I didn't feel like eating so Maggie brought me a sandwich to have when I was peckish."

Mitsy nodded and smiled. "I'll leave you in peace then. Let me know if you want company," she said.

4

Wedding Plans

Pete and Jackie's wedding had been deferred because of the restrictions that everyone had been living under during the covid pandemic. It was disappointing, but both believed that as it had taken them so long to find each other, a few more months would not matter.

As it had turned out, serendipity had played a part in the couple meeting each other in the first place. Pete's mother Mitsy had suggested to Jackie's father Arthur that the hotel Pete used for a good local stop-over when he was visiting her at Appledore House might be useful for Jackie. This was how the two met by chance over a hotel breakfast before visiting their elderly parents. Subsequently Jackie had helped Pete by researching Mitsy's father's music career, which was the sort of thing she did for a living. It was a rather long distance romance, with Jackie living in London and Pete in Dublin but as Pete's work required him to travel extensively, he managed a London stop-over at regular intervals.

More recently, the couple had started to phone Appledore House on a Sunday afternoon. First, they called Mitsy and then phoned Arthur. Often Pete and Jackie were together in either Pete's flat in Dublin or at Jackie's in London. Once Appledore House residents were permitted to mix again, Arthur started to call in to see Mitsy and then it became a four-way video call.

Eventually, it seemed that it might be safe to proceed with the nuptials and on one of their Sunday calls Pete was delighted to announce the date and the venue. The couple had decided to marry at Camden Registry Office as it was close to Jackie's flat in London. This would be convenient for them and was also helpfully located near Kings Cross Station so that their parents could travel down for the wedding by train.

Mitsy was immediately delegated the task of finding out how she and Arthur would travel. Before long she had booked their train tickets on line and asked if Greg, the gardener, would be able to take them to the station and collect them much later the same day. Given Mitsy's unfortunate experience when she was locked in the disused Anderson shelter at the bottom of the garden, which was partly caused by Greg and his son unwittingly sealing off the doorway with a large mill stone, she felt that anything he could do to atone for his error of judgment would be helpful!

Misty had planned for them to travel from nearby Bradford Interchange but this involved one change later in the journey, so she opted for the Leeds to London train instead. This would take them directly to King's Cross station without the need for any delay from changing trains en route. It turned out that if they set off early enough, they could arrive before midday so they would be in good time for the afternoon ceremony.

Jackie had invited a school friend Jess and her husband to act as witnesses. Pete did not invite anyone as he was happy to have just his mother and future father-in-law there, so the whole event would be quite a modest affair. It was agreed that no one else in the family would be involved as they preferred to focus on 'tying the knot.' Both Pete and Jackie had attended weddings of friends that had turned into a major worry and diplomatic planning exercise, not to mention considerable expense. Mitsy had agreed wholeheartedly as she knew that her sister Sky would find some way to steal the limelight and make a scene if they did invite her. It would be safer to tell her after the event!

To begin with, Jackie was rather concerned to find that her husband-to-be had booked Camden Registry Office which was situated in the local Town Hall. She was aware that the Town Hall had recently been renovated at great expense and was reputed to offer a lavish main venue hall seating over fifty people. This had been described in the local paper as the Heath Suite. On further investigation, they found that a smaller, more intimate room was also on offer.

The four of them discussed the plan for the day and they agreed that no one really wanted a formal event. Finally, it was agreed that they would all have a light lunch after the ceremony at Jackie's before Mitsy and Arthur caught the 16:33 train back. The following weekend it was proposed that the newlyweds would visit Mitsy and Arthur and take them out for a meal to complete the celebration.

Mitsy had already discussed with Arthur what they should wear and what would be appropriate as a wedding gift. All they needed was good weather, no risk of covid spoiling the event and the day would be perfect!

Over the time that Mitsy and Arthur had both lived at Appledore House, they had grown to like and respect each other. Mitsy was prone to having mishaps and adventures and Arthur was often called upon to keep an eye on his friend.

Opposite the care home there had been an old mill building which Mitsy had unwisely decided to visit during the night. She had not been able to resist her curiosity once she had seen shadowy figures in what was thought to be an empty building. While there, she had been amazed to see ghostly mill-workers. They did not appear to see her but she was able to see for herself what dreadful working conditions they experienced in the nineteenth century.

Unfortunately, she was unable to get back inside Appledore House without getting soaking wet in a thunderstorm and attracting the wrath of Mrs P, the co-owner of Appledore House. If the truth were told, you could not have a more kind and considerate care home owner but of course Mrs Podsiadlo was concerned that Mitsy could have come to real harm that night over in the disused mill building.

It was Arthur who initiated the search party the next time Mitsy went missing and although she was only locked in the gardeners' refuge everyone was all too aware that an unintended night out of doors for an older person could lead to hypothermia.

Mitsy was well-liked by most of the other residents at Appledore House. She was respected for her 'joie de vivre' and insatiable curiosity, and she had at various times made use of her lively imagination by writing a book, completing a vibrant oil painting, and initiating research into family ancestry. She was prone to getting bored and this was not helped by the stringent lock down regulations during the early days of the covid pandemic.

Having a wedding for her and Arthur to prepare for, was a least a short term distraction of which she took full advantage.

A chance comment on last Sunday's family phone call revealed that Jackie intended to keep her own name and just add Pete's surname to it when they were married. So, she would become Mrs Benson-Howard. She thought it would be easier for people who knew her only through her work at the British Film Institute. Mitsy was not so sure about this. 'I was happy to take Peter's name when we married,' she mumbled. As Pete did not seem concerned, she kept her thoughts to herself.

5

The Mystery Unfolds

That afternoon, Mitsy began to think about what she had noticed earlier in the day. First, a man peering at the signature on an oil painting in the hall and then a woman studying the pottery vases in the dining room.

As she thought about it, she berated herself for being so uncharacteristically unobservant. 'How is it that I've lived at Appledore House for all this time and I hadn't noticed the paintings or the china ornaments?' She sighed to herself. 'I suppose when I moved in, I was far too preoccupied with moving from my family home to a strange place. At the time, I was concerned about losing my independence and worrying so much about how Pete would have to sell the house in order to pay for me moving in here.'

Mitsy's room was at the back of the building and overlooked the attractive garden. It had been her priority in terms of settling in. She made sure that she had a desk for her laptop and that there was a wardrobe and a chest of drawers for her clothes and a bookcase. Having a few of her own things around her helped her to feel more at home.

The more Mitsy reflected, the more she was puzzled by the strange man and woman looking at paintings and ornaments. 'I wonder what is so special about them?' she asked herself.

She concluded that this mystery needed some discreet investigation. Picking up a pad of yellow post-it notes and a pen, she left her room and walked nonchalantly along the corridor. Apart from carrying the wherewithal to make notes, she had also mentally prepared herself with an alibi. If she saw any of the residents or staff members and they asked where she was going, she would say she was popping in to see Maggie to check if her monthly payments to Appledore House were up-to-date.

Maggie had done a sterling job as matron and boss of Appledore House since Mrs Podsiadlo had moved to Gerald Longhope's care home for those with dementia. Mitsy had always got on well with her, especially since she had detected a member of staff stealing money from the residents. Maggie found Mitsy quite an enigma; her insistence that she regularly saw a ghost in the building seemed so fanciful but in many other ways she seemed to have her feet on the ground.

Approaching the painting in the hallway, just inside the front door, Mitsy glanced up and down and decided that the coast was clear. The painting, now she looked more closely, seemed to be a quality oil painting which featured an attractive seascape with coastline and beach. A small signature was just about visible in the bottom right hand corner which credited the work to Helena Krajewska. Quickly, Mitsy jotted down the name and tucked the note into her pocket.

Next, she headed towards the dining room. There, she was surprised to see Billy, one of the part-time kitchen staff. He was slowly wiping the cutlery with a tea-towel. Mitsy, skilled at diverting attention when this was needed, walked straight in, and asked "Billy, have you seen Raymond this morning?"

Billy smiled. "I think he came in for an early breakfast, Mitsy," he said. Of course, Mitsy knew this but at least it appeared to explain her presence in the dining room mid-morning.

"That's good. Thank you, Billy. You look busy!" At the same time as these pronouncements, Mitsy casually picked up the vase that she had seen the unknown young woman handling. "This is pretty. I don't think I have seen it before."

Turning it up to look underneath, she commented, "Oh it's Clarice Cliff. There's a signature here" and placing it back on the sideboard, she turned to Billy again "well, thank you very much. I'll leave you to your spoon polishing!"

Back in her room, Mitsy carefully noted her findings in a new note book. After a coffee and a biscuit, she turned to her computer to make good use of the search engine or 'Mr Google' as she liked to call it.

Half an hour later, Mitsy had carried out her research and made some notes.

> *Helena Krajewska born 1910 died 1998 Warsaw. Mid-20th century Polish realist/impressionist artist, worked in oils. A similar painting like this seascape is currently worth £1,400*
>
> *Clarice Cliff born 1899 died 1972 English ceramic artist based in Tunstall, Stoke on Trent. A vase in the 'Bizarre' range worth £70+*

'Well,' said Mitsy to herself. 'There's more to this than meets the eye.' She decided that she should carefully identify the paintings and decorative china spread all around the house in the public areas. Apart from relying on 'Mr Google' she would need to learn more about these items and this could involve watching 'Antiques Roadshow' and several other relevant television programmes. Mitsy was easily bored and was always on the look-out for a new project, especially if it gave her a chance to learn new things.

She thought fleetingly about her own painting project, when she had dabbled in oil painting a year or so ago. She glanced up to her wall where the sole evidence of those endeavours was hanging. She still liked it and thought maybe she would start a new painting some time. Of course, Raymond who lived opposite was a much more skilled artist but he preferred to keep his talent to himself.

Never one to delay getting started on a new project, she turned on the television and immersed herself in learning about the various items on offer in 'The Bidding Room'. By the end of the programme, she had a new page full of neatly written notes about all manner of objects and furniture, as well as estimated values and the price eventually agreed by the experts.

Satisfied with her work, she decided to wash and change ready for dinner. This was one of Mitsy's habits that had continued even after she had retired from work. Given that she had worked mainly in the retail sector including a pharmacy, all of which were clean places, it wasn't really necessary to change her clothes after work but for her this neatly punctuated daytime and evening.

When the dinner bell rang, she was ready to meet up with the other residents to chat about the day. She decided that she would keep to herself the puzzle of the unknown couple who had been scrutinising things around the home, until she had some answers.

6

The New Normal

Mitsy was wary of everyone who tried to insist that the pandemic was over when clearly there were many people who were still affected by the virus. Although most news reports appeared to be playing it down, the data on the number of people ill or dying was still available on the government website if, like Mitsy, you knew where to look.

An email from her sister Sky highlighted the point. It seemed that Sky's husband Jim had caught covid and had been seriously unwell for three weeks. True to Sky's nature, her comments concentrated on how this was his own fault – for going in to work – and how much his illness had affected her. Sky had called upon her two daughters to help look after him as it was 'all too much' for her. In the last sentence of the email, she mentioned as an apparent afterthought, that Jim's elderly aunt had died after catching the virus in her care home in Kent and her neighbour was suffering from long covid. 'Hmm. This is very far from over,' said Mitsy to herself.

She was sad to know that Jim had been ill. He was a kind and thoughtful man who was a reliable mainstay of the household; she often wondered how he managed to cope with Sky and her constant complaining.

She wrote a reply immediately to her sister, reassuring her that she was well, not that Sky had enquired, and hoping that Jim would be feeling much better soon.

Just as she was contemplating whether to describe how Appledore House had taken precautions or to mention Lucy's death from covid, the phone rang. It was Elaine, Mitsy's friend who lived nearby.

"Now we are all back to normal I thought you might like to come round for coffee on Friday," she said. "I've got loads to tell you and it would be good to see you, at last."

Mitsy explained that she had only just started going out again and all the residents had been advised to wear a mask indoors. Her recent lunch in the pub garden had worked well, so she suggested they had an outdoor coffee. Elaine sounded a bit deflated but agreed that they would have an al fresco coffee if it did not rain.

Checking her diary, which had hardly any entries this year, Mitsy realised that next week would be one year since Jackie and Pete got engaged. 'Oh, I do like anniversaries,' she said to herself, as she checked her collection of spare cards for all such situations. She did not have anything absolutely right for the occasion so she picked a blank card showing two affectionate rabbits, hoping that would suffice.

As there was nothing else to do, she decided to walk across the road to take the card to the post box. Affixing a postage stamp to the envelope, she wondered if the stamps would soon have an image of King Charles III on them. Not that she was a royalist particularly, although everyone at Appledore House had watched the coronation on the television. To be truthful, Mitsy didn't watch much at all, just the bits shown on the news while they were all having a celebration tea and cakes in the residents' lounge.

Back indoors, as she headed towards her room, Mitsy noticed three small vases on a shelf over the radiator. 'I'm sure I've not seen those before either,' she observed, as she picked up each of them and made a mental note to investigate Moorcroft pottery later.

As she opened the door to her own room, a middle-aged couple came out of room five next door. Mitsy recognised Norma's daughter and her husband. She immediately offered her condolences.

"Oh, hello Mitsy. We have the rather sad task of clearing Norma's belongings today," she said. "Maggie said that we needed to take away anything personal and the things we don't want will go in a skip so they can redecorate the room."

Mitsy was all too aware of the process after someone dies at Appledore House but as she didn't want to add to the couple's distress, she just kept her silence.

Back in her room, she remembered to investigate the Moorcroft pottery that she had spotted in the hallway. It seemed that William Moorcroft was born in 1872 into a family of potters. He pursued some serious art studies before deciding he would prefer a practical career rather than an academic one.

His pieces were recognisable by the attractive colours he used along with a technique he introduced which is known as tube-lining. Mitsy realised that there were too many different designs for her to remember although she had a feeling the vases in the hall could include Poppy, Crocus and Hibiscus patterns. This was when she realised that all she needed to do was to take a surreptitious photo of the items with her phone so that she could compare them against the pictures on the internet later.

There was a knock on the door. Norma's daughter stood there with a glass vase in her hand. "We just wondered if you would like this to put your flowers in, Mitsy, and as a keepsake from Norma. She was fond of you and I'm sure she would wish you to have something. "

"Oh. How kind. Yes, I would love to have something to remember Norma by."

She took the attractive frosted glass vase and placed it on the top of her bookcase. Later, she consulted Mr Google and much to her surprise it appeared that the vase came from the workshop of Rene Lalique. Mitsy was not sure if it was genuine, but the mark on the bottom suggested that it was.

She smiled to think that barely a week ago she had a limited knowledge of antiques but since she had started to learn what she could from on-line antique experts as well as those on several TV programmes, she was beginning to recognise famous names.

That evening, when Joyce came round with the evening medication, she admired the new vase. Mitsy explained where it had come from. "It will be nice to have something to remind me of Norma. You know, I hadn't really noticed before, Joyce, but we have some pretty pieces of pottery around the house as well as some interesting oil paintings."

"Oh yes," said Joyce, "Mr P was quite the collector."

Mitsy was not sure how this related to the former owner of Appledore House and looked rather puzzled.

"When Mr and Mrs Podsiadlo took on the care home, it was empty and all the rooms were bare. Mr P started to go to local auctions to buy furniture as it was cheaper than going to a furniture shop and in any case post-war there wasn't much around. I think he also picked up job lots of china and cutlery and once they had got the place the way they wanted it, he just kept on going to the auctions. It was quite a hobby for him."

Joyce liked Mitsy and although she didn't often have time to chat with all the residents during the medication round, she did sometimes make an exception.

Mitsy spent the rest of the evening trying to find out more about her Lalique vase. She concluded that it was really valuable and thus too good to fill with water and cut flowers so she found a permanent spot for it on a high shelf where it would not get knocked over.

Her notes on antiques were turning into quite a document and now Joyce's information about how most of them came into the house had added to the interest.

7

Elaine

The sun was shining mid-morning on Friday, so Mitsy was happy that her invitation to have coffee with Elaine would take place in her garden.

Tapping gently on the front door, she was surprised to find that it was opened by a man. In some ways, it was not a surprise because nothing Elaine did could surprise or shock Mitsy any more after some of their shared adventures.

"Hello," said the man. "You must be mum's friend Mitsy? Do come in." Mitsy shook her head as Elaine appeared behind him.

"No that's OK Grant, we're having coffee in the garden."

With that, she waved her hands to indicate the side path round to the back of the house. As Mitsy wandered round slowly, she wracked her brains to remember if she had ever heard Elaine talk about a son called Grant. She had heard about Elaine's other children but she was almost certain that Elaine had never mentioned a son.

Settling down in one of the deck chairs already set out, she waited until Elaine emerged from the back door.

"Oh, its lovely to see you Mitsy. It hasn't been the same having chats on messenger or the occasional phone call, has it? How have you been?"

Mitsy gave a brief summary of how the residents of Appledore House had fared, much of which Elaine already

31

knew. Frankly, not much had happened during the lockdowns that was worth sharing. She mentioned briefly the deaths and illnesses but she preferred to keep the tone of their conversation as light as possible.

"I was pleased to say hello to your son. I'm not sure I know much about him?" said Mitsy, thinking that this would give Elaine an opportunity to tell her all sorts of things.

"Aaaaah. Grant. Yes, well he's been a naughty boy so he's been inside for a while."

Mitsy was rather confused by this, especially as the information had been delivered with a phoney cockney accent. He was already inside the house and as a grown man it wasn't likely that he was being kept prisoner by his mother. She kept quiet, knowing that Elaine couldn't resist telling a story.

Eventually it transpired that 'inside' meant in prison, where Grant had been for several years. Mitsy felt he must have done something very wrong to be incarcerated for such a long time. She felt it was rather rude and intrusive to ask what his crime was, so she asked the next thing that came into her head: "Oh dear. Which prison was he in?"

"Wandsworth nick. I couldn't visit during Covid so we haven't seen each other for ages. But let me tell you my important news!" said Elaine with some enthusiasm as she poured out the coffee from a mid-sixties' coffee pot. Mitsy was privately amused that she was beginning to observe such things with ease. She nodded.

"Well. You remember Martin who is the head chef at the school where I used to work as a dinner lady?"

Mitsy smiled as she recalled how this man regularly pretended to his wife that he was attending a management course, so that he and Elaine could have a sunshine holiday together. She wondered why the abandoned wife never queried how he came home from this work commitment with a suntan.

"Martin has left his wife! I think he wants to move in with me. Well, to be honest I think she might have guessed he was playing around and she has kicked him out."

Mitsy raised her eyebrows but didn't respond. Serial boyfriends, often married to someone else, seemed to be a pattern in Elaine's life.

"Of course, he's got no chance. I'm waiting until he asks and then I'll explain it's not possible as I've got my son here."

Finally, Mitsy managed to get a word in edgeways: "So has your son Grant moved in with you permanently?" she asked.

"Good lord, no. It's only until he gets himself sorted but Martin won't know that."

"You're fond of Martin, though?"

"He's nice enough but I couldn't live with a man that has dirty fingernails."

Somehow that comment put a stop to anything Mitsy could think to say. She could not contemplate how a head chef feeding hundreds of school children daily could have dirty fingernails.

They both stared into their coffee cups imagining Martin and his alleged dirty fingernails. Mitsy really couldn't think of anything helpful to say. Fortunately, Elaine launched into the silence to ask after Pete and Jackie. Mitsy described the forthcoming wedding arrangements.

"Well, that sounds like you have it all fully organised. It's a shame it's so soon, otherwise I would have willingly given you a lift. I shall be taking Grant back to London in a while, once he's got a few things organised."

Mitsy turned her attention to Elaine's garden, which was brimming with attractive flowers, despite appearing rather untidy. Elaine enjoyed gardening but she had some unusual perspectives on gardening activity. She always left weeds until they had flowered and turned to seed, for the benefit of the bees so that they had a regular source of pollen. Seed heads were then supposedly left for the seed-eating birds. She resolutely refused to water any plant, even if it had turned yellow with thirst. This was because if it could not survive the climate in her garden then 'it doesn't deserve to live here' she suggested. Mitsy felt that any mention of climate change would not affect Elaine's thinking on the matter.

"Your garden is looking good, Elaine," said Mitsy.

Elaine cast her eyes over her small patch. "Oh, look. The wind has blown over the roses. Would you like some to put in a vase to cheer up your room?"

For some strange reason, Elaine had very little insight to Appledore House, given that Mitsy did not find her room depressing in any way. She acknowledged the offer and within minutes she was presented with a generous bunch of pale pink roses. It seemed an appropriate time to make her goodbyes and she guessed that Elaine had things to do with Grant as she made no complaint as she walked with her from the back garden to the front gate.

"Let me know how the wedding goes! Take pictures!"

"I will try Elaine. Thank you for the coffee and say goodbye to Grant for me."

Mitsy smiled to herself. Any time she spent with Elaine always left her feeling amused. Whilst she would never dream of sharing the matter of Martin's dirty fingernails with anyone else, it would continue to entertain her.

8

The Wedding Day

Mitsy straightened her hat and smiled at her reflection in the full length mirror. She was genuinely quite excited to be going to her son's wedding. Of course, it would have been so much better if her husband Peter had been alive to see his son get married after all Pete's years of bachelordom but under the circumstances it was rather fitting to be heading off to London shortly with Arthur, father of the bride.

There was a gentle tap at the door and Greg was there, ready to take her and Arthur to the train station. Mitsy checked her handbag, gloves, and the meagre contents of the shopping bag that she was taking for sustenance during the journey. Meanwhile, Arthur appeared, looking very smart in his dark suit. Arthur had mixed feelings about wearing the suit he had bought for Ivy's funeral but it did not really make sense to buy a new suit just for one day. Of course, Arthur had given his daughter Jackie away before, but sadly that marriage had not lasted. He was feeling very hopeful that marriage to Mitsy's son Pete was a much better prospect.

Greg headed out to his car, keen to ensure that his two passengers would be comfortable for the short journey to the station. He was not quite sure how to converse with Mitsy, given that she had recently got trapped inside the old air-raid shelter that he used as a garden shed at the bottom of the garden. It was, of course, a simple error not to have checked there was no one inside before he and his son rolled the large millstone in front of the door. After all, what sensible person would go into a pitch-dark building for no reason? Greg had worked for many years at Appledore House, and when he was not keeping the garden under control or harvesting the fruit and vegetables he raised for the care home, he was happy to do any odd jobs. He was often to be seen chatting to the residents but he was a little uncertain as to how Mitsy would see him now that she had discovered his collection of rather dubious and exotic gentlemen's magazines. He concluded that the less said about that the better.

The roads were quiet at this time of the morning and it did not take as long as he had expected to get to Leeds station. Greg pulled up at the taxi rank at the front, as that seemed a good place to stop in order to give Mitsy and Arthur easy access to their train. After checking with Mitsy the expected time of the train they would return on, and promising to be there to pick them up, Greg jumped out to open the doors of his car with a flourish, just like he had seen hotel commissaires do on the television.

Mitsy and Arthur thanked Greg and headed across the concourse to find out which platform their train would be standing at. Mitsy was giggling. "I was wondering if Greg was going to salute us," she said. They walked slowly as Arthur had decided it was best to take his walking stick to steady his steps because it was likely to be a long and tiring day.

Thankfully, all of Mitsy's careful planning including the on-line ticket purchase came to fruition without a hitch and they were speedily directed to their platform. When the train arrived a few minutes later, they were delighted to find that they were in a quiet carriage with only a few other passengers. Although Mitsy did not say it, she did hope that they would not be subjected to screaming children or teenagers listening to noisy music. As it turned out, because it was an early train, the passengers all seemed quite serious and bound for work so they too were hoping for a peaceful journey.

Not long after the train set off, Arthur and Mitsy started to quietly point out to each other some places that they knew or had heard of. The train's first stop was Halifax and as they approached, it was easy to spot Wainhouse Tower and many of the old mill properties.

As they began to relax, Mitsy brought out from her shopping bag a bottle of water. "Would you like a drink, Arthur?"

"Not at the moment, thank you Mitsy. I might wander along to the restaurant car for a coffee perhaps. I'll get one for you too, of course."

They had eaten breakfast earlier than usual because of the time they had to leave and Mitsy was already feeling peckish. She brought out a packet of crisps from her bag which she shared with Arthur.

Just as the train left Halifax, a ticket collector walked through, checking tickets as she went. She enquired in a friendly manner if they were having a special day out and Arthur was pleased to tell her that they were going to London for his daughter's wedding.

Next, they passed through Wakefield and again the historic buildings stood out against the skyline.

"Wakefield has been designated City of Culture in 2025," said Mitsy.

"How do you know these things?" asked Arthur, although he realised that Mitsy always watched the Look North news on the television and read the local paper. He realised, almost too late, that Mitsy was still harbouring a grudge against the local journalist who insisted on emphasising Mitsy's age when reporting on the author of **Violet's Story**, the novel she had written which was set in Appledore House. Quickly, before she could say anything about local papers or journalists, Arthur decided to fetch coffees for them both and headed off in the direction that the ticket collector had indicated.

Arthur was missing for a long time and Mitsy was just beginning to wonder what had happened to him when he appeared, smiling, with two steaming coffees and a couple of packets of ginger biscuits.

Before long the train passed through Pontefract and by that stage Mitsy and Arthur were chatting away and not really following the route any more.

Arthur was keen to tell Mitsy how happy he was that Jackie would be marrying Pete. They agreed that the couple seemed to have hit it off from the day they met. Given that they had managed to maintain a long distance relationship with one of them in Dublin and the other in London, not to mention the difficulties and loneliness of surviving lockdown alone in different countries, it augured well for the future.

Mitsy responded by saying that her son Pete was obviously 'choosy' having not found a suitable candidate to be his wife before now.

The conversation drifted off onto other subjects, mainly around events at Appledore House and so neither of them noticed how quickly the journey was passing until the train stopped at Doncaster station.

Mitsy consulted her notebook and announced they had better start getting ready for arrival in London. Both decided to make use of the toilet, which was a shaky experience as the train was hurtling along at high speed. They took it in turns to use the toilet in order to keep their seats and belongings safe. Mitsy returned after she had checked her makeup and Arthur said that he needed to comb his hair, not that Mitsy thought it was necessary!

As the train pulled into Kings Cross station, Mitsy noted that it was eleven o'clock and thus the train was precisely on time. Even better, she could see Pete at the end of the platform, waiting for them.

Within minutes all three had negotiated the short walk to Jackie's flat. After hugs and kisses all round, they were treated to another coffee. Then Jess and her husband Olaf arrived and they were left to talk to Mitsy and Arthur while Jackie and Pete went to get changed into their wedding clothes.

As it was the first time that Mitsy had been to Jackie's flat, she was content to look around discretely and she recognised various items that had come from Pete's home in Dublin.

Pete looked very smart in his navy suit, complete with matching waistcoat and crisp white shirt. Mitsy was always proud of her son, especially today. Jackie appeared soon after, wearing a pale pink and blue dress with matching jacket and fascinator. She also carried a box that had just been delivered by the florist with a delicate posy of mixed pink and blue flowers that echoed the colours of her dress. There were matching corsages for Pete and all the guests.

"I think we are almost ready," said Jackie.

"Just a moment," said Mitsy. "I wondered if you would like to wear this necklace?" She carefully lifted a dainty heart-shaped enamelled locket which sat on a velvet choker and held it out to Jackie.

"Oh. That is beautiful!" she said. "How did you manage to find something the same pink as my dress? With pale blue velvet?"

"Ha!" said Mitsy, "you know the saying 'something old, something new, something borrowed, something blue'? Well, I hope this will meet those requirements. Part of it is old and borrowed but I wanted to give it to you, if you like it."

Jackie gave Mitsy a kiss and smiled at Pete. "I couldn't have picked a better mother-in-law," she said.

Then she smiled, "I was thinking we could go across the road now but we're a bit early."

Pete suggested that they could probably walk slowly to the Town Hall, then take some photos outside and that was what they did.

Camden Register Office has an imposing exterior in Judd Street and thus it was an ideal setting to mark the occasion with some photos. By the time everyone had taken a photo for everyone else ("can you do one on my phone now" etc.) it was time to go inside, meet the registrar and proceed with the ceremony.

The room was small but pleasantly decorated. The registrar shook hands with Jackie and Pete and made some comment about music. Pete delved into his smart suit pocket and produced a DVD. Jess, Olaf, Mitsy and Arthur took their seats and within a couple of minutes some charming and restful music began to play. Pete smiled, winked at his mother but Mitsy had no idea what that was about.

Arthur stepped forward to be next to his daughter, Mitsy stood next to Pete and the two witnesses stood to one side.

The music stopped and the familiar words were spoken by the registrar. In a matter of minutes Pete and Jackie were husband and wife, the register was signed and witnessed and several more photos were taken.

Once outside, Jess and Mitsy insisted on throwing confetti and the men were tasked with recording that too. Pete and Jackie held hands, gazed into each other's eyes and everyone applauded.

Back at the house, Jess and Jackie proceeded to organise where everyone would sit, at the same time as bringing out plates and plates of food. Pete fetched some glasses and opened a bottle of champagne noisily. Arthur proposed a toast to the happy couple and to everyone in the room. Jackie thanked everyone for coming and there was a quiet hum of conversation between eating the sandwiches and snacks.

"Did you like the music, Mum?" asked Pete.

Mitsy looked slightly puzzled. "It was nice, and just right for the occasion, but I didn't recognise it."

"Well, it was written by David Thompson," said Pete, grinning.

"Oh! Really!"

Mitsy turned to explain to the others, "That was my father, Pete's grandfather. He was a composer and in fact he was partly responsible for Jackie and Pete meeting."

Jackie joined in, explaining how she had been able to research through her work some of the music that had been recorded for TV and radio. "What was funny was that the piece we played at our wedding came from a radio programme. It was a sort of forerunner to the Archers and the episode was about a family wedding. We thought it quite appropriate!"

Finally, Pete looked at his watch and reminded Arthur and Mitsy that their train home would be leaving in half an hour.

With many hugs and kisses, the parents left, reminding the newly-weds that they planned to visit them 'up North' next weekend. Saying goodbye to Jackie's friends, they hastily made their way to the station.

Both Mitsy and Arthur spent much of the homeward journey asleep; the excitement and champagne affecting them both.

At Leeds station, good as his word, Greg was waiting for them. "How was it?" he asked. "Perfect. Just perfect," said Mitsy and Arthur in unison.

9

Secrets

The day after the wedding, Mitsy learned something about Arthur that she would never have expected. They were both sitting in the garden watching Greg prune the laurel bushes. They were still rather tired from the wedding trip so they didn't have much to talk about.

"You did have a long and interesting career in the carpet trade, didn't you Arthur? You told me all about it some time ago. Did you never wonder what it would be like to do something else?" asked Mitsy.

Arthur smiled. "That's an interesting question Mitsy. Why do you ask?"

"Well, I've done all sorts of things myself, mainly to fit in with Pete's schooling and of course my Peter was away at sea a lot so I was always on the lookout for something new to amuse myself with. I cannot imagine what it would be like to work in the same business for the whole of one's life."

Arthur smiled again and looked over to where Greg was working, almost as if he was trying to decide how to answer Mitsy. They sat quietly for a few minutes, then Arthur looked directly at Mitsy with a cheeky grin.

"If you are very good Mitsy, I will tell you a secret."

Mitsy's eyes lit up. She was always ready for a story and, as Arthur knew all too well, she was the soul of discretion.

"OK. I did have another career but no one, not even Ivy knew about it."

Mitsy's face took on a serious expression as she realised that this was something important to Arthur.

"In my last year at University, I was approached by a man who asked if I would be interested in some business trips to other countries, with all expenses paid. At the time, I was intrigued but rather naïve. I agreed to give the job a try and to let him know if I liked it. I wasn't told what the job involved and, with hindsight, he could have been getting me involved in drug-running or something illegal."

"Oh Arthur, how exciting!"

"Well. First of all I had to sign some official papers to say that I would not divulge to anyone, ever, what I did. It seemed that I would be working for a secret branch of the government, I think. Then I was given a new passport. It was my photo (I've no idea how they got that) but a different name and details. The man, whose name I never found out, handed me an envelope with a train ticket, a cross-channel ferry ticket, more train tickets, and typed details of two hotels I had to stay in. The instructions were to travel to the indicated destination and wait for someone to contact me. He was to give me a very small packet which I was to guard with my life and bring it back."

"Oh wow!" said Mitsy, under her breath, "what happened?"

"The trip turned out much as I expected. I saw a couple of capital cities and had some pleasant meals in top hotels. That was all. When I got back, the man who invited me to carry out this assignment met me in the local park and I gave him the tiny packet without the faintest idea what was in it."

"And then what happened?"

"Oh, a month or so later he got in touch with me again. He asked if I enjoyed the trip, which I did. He then said he had another assignment for me if I wanted to do it. I wasn't really sure because I did not know what I was getting into. I said that I did not want to do it if it was bringing something illegal into the country. The man said that it was quite the opposite and that I was helping the country by bringing information that would be helpful to the government in the event of a war."

Arthur smiled. "I decided I would do it again, at least one more time, as it was quite an adventure for a young lad like myself."

"And did you?"

"Well, Mitsy as it turned out, I did several trips to different places. Each time I was to bring a very small package home with me. I have a feeling it was a roll of film but I don't know. Anyway, a few months after this I met Ivy but of course I did not tell her about these business trips. I was having too much fun taking her out so when the man approached me again, I told him I didn't want to do it anymore. He asked for the spare passport back, which I gave him. I never saw him again."

"Wow. That's amazing. I would never have imagined that you were a spy!" said Mitsy with a grin.

Arthur looked round the garden again. "Please don't ever tell anyone this Mitsy. I honestly don't know what I was getting involved with. But, since you asked if I'd ever had any other job, that's the truth."

"Of course not. I won't even mention it again, but thank you for sharing your secret life with me."

"You can see now, why I got the travel bug and how the carpet business came about?"

"Indeed I can. What an amazing experience you had."

Arthur looked at his watch. "Well, I am expecting Jackie to call this afternoon and I'd like to be in my room so I don't miss her."

"Of course. Please give her my love."

"See you later, Mitsy," he said over his shoulder, as he strolled across the grass back into the house.

10

London-bound Again

For the next few days, every time either Mitsy or Arthur went into the lounge or the dining room, at least one of the residents asked to see the wedding photos. Most of the staff had already admired the pictures of the happy couple as well as commenting how smart Mitsy and Arthur looked. Mitsy was pleased she had worn that navy suit with the cerise piping; it was attractive as well as being comfortable. Added to which, she now knew that the colours were right for her!

She found the whole experience of travelling to London and back in a day somewhat exhausting, as had Arthur. They agreed it would be preferable in future for Pete and Jackie to visit them at Appledore House when the couple were free to do so. The plan to come up to see them the following weekend had to be deferred because Pete had business to attend to in The Hague and would not be back until very late on Friday. Another date was agreed and Arthur re-arranged the lunch for the four of them which he had previously booked at The Standsfield Arms.

Mitsy phoned her friend Elaine to give her an update on the wedding. Elaine was pleased to know that it all went well and she was keen to share her news. It seemed that she had not heard any more from Martin the school chef, once she had told him that her son had moved in with her. "Of course, he hasn't really moved in, he's just staying here until he can sort out a flat in London now that he's out of prison."

For a week or two, life settled back into the old routine. Arthur visited a friend who lived in Wakefield, Mitsy had her coffee mornings with Elaine and they resumed their weekly lunch at the pub. They rarely saw people wearing face masks and it did feel more like it used to be before the pandemic.

One day, Mitsy was waiting to watch a TV programme that was likely to show their part of Bradford, and possibly Appledore House. Several of the residents were meeting in the TV lounge and Maggie had promised to join them. Invariably the first to arrive, Mitsy was looking around the room when she noticed the china dog. For once she had her phone with her, so she hastily took a photo of it before anyone else arrived.

The half-hour programme was not especially inspiring. The camera rapidly panned past the frontage of the care home before anyone had time to see it properly and then focussed on the apartments across the road. These had been recently renovated and adapted from an old cotton mill. A few people were aware that Mitsy had ventured into the old mill one night, but they were all too polite to mention her escapade. The remainder of the programme showed the Alhambra Theatre and other well-known sights from the city.

Back in her room, Mitsy remembered that she had taken a photo of the ornament that was in the resident's lounge. A few minutes' search on the laptop and Mitsy had a new entry for her antiques notebook.

Porcelain Staffordshire dog in copper lustre made in 1860 matching pair valued at £195; single? £

She thought it might be worth looking around the house in case there was a second dog as she guessed that one from a pair would not be worth as much two.

Suddenly, the phone rang. "Mitsy, it's Elaine here. I was just wondering if you would come to London with me next week?"

After Mitsy's recent tiring day trip to London by train she was on the verge of declining the invitation when Elaine interrupted her: "I'll be driving down to drop off Grant, as he's found a flat. It's between Streatham and Brixton. It has been nice having him stay but I shall be glad to have my home to myself again. Anyway, I'm happy to do the driving but it would be so much nicer to have your company, especially for the return journey."

Mitsy felt she could not refuse, as Elaine had been a good friend to her since she moved in to Appledore House and she had never once asked a favour of Mitsy.

They discussed when this journey would be and Elaine said she would prepare a flask of coffee and sandwiches. All that was needed was for Mitsy to inform a member of staff that she planned to be out for the day.

Thus it was that Mitsy slipped out of the house at eight-thirty in the morning as they had agreed. Elaine was all ready to go and Grant was not far behind. It seemed that Grant would sit in front as he had long legs. Mitsy was not too happy about this as she tended to feel travel sick in the back seat of cars if she could not see directly ahead. None-the-less, the three of them set off for their 'road trip' with the minimum of delay. Mitsy had already noticed that since Grant had moved in with his mother, Elaine was beginning to use various Americanisms or words that more properly would be found in rap music. It made her smile.

There was not much to see once they were on the M1 motorway; only the back of Grant's head and a never-ending line of traffic. Grant and Elaine chatted away, while Mitsy felt somewhat excluded from the conversation. She could barely hear what they were talking about and when she did catch a phrase or two, she had no idea of the context.

From time to time, Mitsy nodded off to sleep. Each time she woke up she felt nauseous until she sat up straight, breathed deeply, focussed her line of sight between the two front seats and waited until her balance returned to normal. The drive seemed interminable.

After what seemed like several hours, although it was barely two, Elaine appeared to be turning off the motorway. Mitsy could see that they were heading for the services at Watford Gap. In fact, they pulled into the petrol station and alongside the pumps. Elaine at last appeared to acknowledge Mitsy's presence and asked if she wanted to use the toilets. This was truly a relief for her, in both senses, and she extracted herself from the back of the car, breathed in deeply and promptly fell over.

"Good grief, Mitsy. What ever happened?" asked Elaine.

Mitsy brushed away her concerns and suggested maybe her legs had got a bit numb sitting in the same position for so long.

"Right. Well, I'll fill up with diesel, use the loo and then we will be on our way. It's not far now."

Mitsy thought this last pronouncement was rather optimistic but said nothing.

In fact, it was not long before they turned off the M1 and the satnav started to give directions towards their destination. Elaine was rather pleased with herself as she had not made a good job of route finding when using this technology previously. She also began to include Mitsy in the conversation, which made the journey pass more quickly, it seemed.

Eventually, they arrived in a wide tree-lined road with large Victorian brick-built houses. Grant peered closely at every house until he spotted number 158. "Here. Here it is!"

Elaine realised that all the parking spaces were for residents only, but she reverse-parked into a small space and said, "We're not stopping, you know. We've got a long way to go back."

Mitsy moved into the front seat and after Elaine had just "popped up" to see Grant's flat they set off again barely ten minutes after they had arrived.

The first part of the return journey was conducted in silence as Elaine needed to concentrate on the traffic, getting into the correct lane and following the dulcet tones of the satnav woman.

Once they were back on the M1 again, Elaine began to relax. "I must say Grant's flat doesn't look too bad. I was worried he was going to end up in a squat again but he said he must have a proper address for the probation officer to check."

Mitsy felt at a bit of a loss, not knowing anything about the crime, the penalty, or the aftermath.

Mitsy ventured, "Do you think he will be able to keep out of trouble now?" It was a bit risky but she wanted to find some way to get Elaine to talk. This did the trick and suddenly the floodgates opened.

"Yes, I feel better about things this time."

Mitsy wondered privately how many times Grant had been in prison.

"Last time he got in with a bad lot and they all ended up in a squat and growing cannabis."

"It must be worrying for you," said Mitsy. She reflected privately how fortunate she was that her Pete had gone from university, to the Civil Service, to working for the European Commission. He had never once asked for money, support or somewhere to live. Of course, Pete may have done some bad things she was not aware of, but somehow, she doubted it. In fact, Pete had been a tower of strength after his father, Peter had died and he dealt with selling the family home and arranging for his mother to move into Appledore House.

As they headed further north Elaine seemed to relax and chat more naturally.

"You know, Mitsy, when Grant first got into trouble, I thought it was teenage misbehaviour but I'm inclined to think it's in his genes. Not that his dad Reg was a bad man, but he wasn't totally trustworthy."

Mitsy felt she could not comment, knowing what she did about Elaine's numerous men friends including the illicit holidays with Martin over the years.

As it was, Elaine seemed more comfortable sharing information about Grant as the journey continued.

"This latest stretch ('she really does know the lingo,' thought Mitsy) he was done for GBH and handling stolen goods. The silly fella left his finger prints on some jewellery that came from a big house on Wimbledon Common and in the same week he got a bit handy with a man in the pawn shop. He never used to have a temper but fortunately he didn't do too much damage and the man was only in hospital overnight."

Mitsy was at a loss to know how to react to these revelations but as she looked across at Elaine's dashboard, she noticed a red light was showing.

"Elaine, did you know your oil warning light is on?"

"Oh yeah, it's been on for ages. I think it will go off by the time we get home."

"But Elaine, you're not supposed to drive with it on. I think you are supposed to pull over and call the AA or the RAC or something."

While Elaine was shaking her head casually at what she deemed an unnecessary fuss, they both realised that smoke was starting to come out from under the car bonnet.

"Pull over, Elaine. Pull over onto the hard shoulder!"

Elaine appeared to take no notice but by this stage, Mitsy was shouting at the top of her voice: "STOP!! For God's sake stop! Pull over!"

As they slowly rolled to a halt, Mitsy flung open the passenger door, grabbed hold of Elaine's arm and pulled her roughly towards the outside. As this involved Elaine scrambling over the gear lever, it turned into an ungainly mix of legs and arms.

"RIGHT!" shouted Mitsy. "We have to go up that bank and stand out of the way of the car or any other vehicles."

Clinging on to Elaine's arm and dragging her somewhat unwillingly up the grassy bank, they were both horrified to hear a WHOOMPH behind them as Elaine's car burst into flames.

They sat down shakily on the bank, both too shocked to speak. It had all happened so quickly that there had been little time to think. The car burned ferociously, sending thick smoke billowing across the motorway. The traffic started to slow down and they could see people craning their necks to see what had happened.

After a few minutes a car with a flashing blue light appeared and as it approached, they could hear it was also sounding its siren. The police car drove on the hard shoulder, carefully avoiding the traffic that had now backed up on all three lanes of the motorway.

"Right, ladies. Is anyone hurt? Is there anyone else in the vehicle?"

Elaine shook her head.

"And which of you is the owner of the vehicle?"

Elaine wordlessly indicated it was herself.

Before any more questions could be asked, a fire engine hurtled up, also using the hard shoulder. Nothing was said, two uniformed men just stepped down from their fire engine and carefully unreeled a hose. A third fireman checked with the policeman that Elaine's car was empty, before they proceeded to douse it with water.

Mitsy noticed that hazard warning lights were flashing on many of the cars held up by their conflagration.

It seemed to take only a few minutes to put out the fire, during which time the policeman had radioed for incident signs to be switched on and had reassured Elaine and Mitsy that cars catch on fire all the time and can be caused by a fuel leak, electrical fault, or a damaged rubber hose.

Elaine started to cry when she realised that her car would never be driveable again. Mitsy suggested that she would probably be covered by insurance, although that did not seem to be much compensation for the shock and distress caused.

The policeman asked how far it was to their home and explained that he would not be able to offer a taxi service.

"That's alright," said Mitsy, taking control of the situation. "If you could take us to somewhere safe to stop, such as a service station, we will phone Appledore House where I live and I'm sure someone would come to collect us."

Neither of them had been paying much attention to the road or where they were, because they had been chatting so much, but the policeman said that there was a service station only a couple of miles away.

And so it was that within twenty minutes Elaine and Mitsy were sitting at Woolley Edge services, drinking coffee, and waiting for the ever helpful Greg who had been pressed into service again by Maggie, to collect the stranded women. The fire brigade was making sure that the fire was fully extinguished and the policeman had arranged for a pickup truck to remove the blackened shell of what had been Elaine's car.

"Well," said Mitsy. "That was an experience I wouldn't want to repeat, but at least we are both safe and sound."

11

Any Port in a Storm

After their ill-fated road trip, Mitsy phoned Elaine the next morning to check that she had recovered from the shock of her car catching fire. It seemed that she had already been in touch with her insurance company who said they would send an assessor out to look at her car, or what remained of it. Elaine was certain that it would be considered a write-off and had enquired how she was to manage in the meantime. Accordingly, the company were arranging for a hire car for Elaine to use until she received the compensation. "It won't cover the cost of another car," she confided to Mitsy. "Maybe I'll have to put up with Martin after all."

Mitsy believed that if Elaine invited Martin to move in with her just because he had a car, this episode would not end well, but she had learned over the years not to offer advice, especially when it was not asked for. Instead, she agreed to go round for a coffee later, even though it wasn't their usual day.

Her next task – why was it that life seemed to comprise one job after another? - was to write to Sky to tell her that Pete and Jackie had got married in London. She felt sure that Sky would be offended not to have been invited but Mitsy thought it was best to let her know shortly after the event, ascribing the reason for such a small gathering to covid. In any case, she was not sure if her brother-in-law had recovered from his bout of the virus so she assumed he could still be contagious.

Looking out of her window for inspiration while attempting to compose this letter, she realised that a pair of golden eyes were staring at her. Mitsy blinked and then smiled. "Hello, Puss," she said to the open window. The visiting black cat had found a way of sitting just outside Mitsy's window, on some recently discarded seed boxes. Mitsy assumed these had been placed there temporarily by Greg or his son.

She could hear the cat was purring quietly so she got up to give her a stroke. Mitsy herself had shared her home with several cats in the past; all were called Puss, some even had regnal numbers. She enjoyed it when cats from nearby houses visited Appledore House – it made the place feel more homely. Her own cat had crossed over the rainbow bridge not long before she moved to Appledore House.

Once she had finished her letter to Sky, she changed her slippers for shoes and took her coat out of the wardrobe so that she could walk to the letter box. Although she could quite easily have sent Sky an email, she thought that a pretty notelet with a carefully thought through explanation would be more acceptable. She realised that emails can easily be deleted unintentionally, whereas a letter can be read and reread over several days. She sometimes wondered why she had to tip-toe around her sister's sensitivity but she knew the reason really was because Sky could be quite nasty if she did not agree with you.

Walking down the corridor, she could hear a bit of a commotion in the hallway. She could see that there were three women, standing in a huddle, around a large set of suitcases. Their noisy chatter suggested that there was something wrong.

Mitsy, always helpful and just a little curious as to what this was all about, said: "Hello! Does anyone need any help?"

They explained that they were moving in to Appledore House temporarily until the flood waters around their care home receded. Of course, Mitsy was aware of the torrential rain that different parts of the country had experienced recently. In fact, she had considered that it might have been a blessing if the heavy rains had come a week later and maybe doused the horrible fire that engulfed Elaine's car. But she really had not anticipated flooding on the scale that would drive people from their homes.

Just as Mitsy was responding to this information, Maggie came hurrying along the corridor and proceeded to speak to them all.

"Ah, Mitsy. You can help here. Would you be kind enough to show Meena to her room? She will be staying in room five." Maggie directed the other two ladies towards the lift where, Mitsy presumed, they would be taken to two empty rooms.

"Meena, I'll take one of your bags and you can come with me. It's not far," said Mitsy. "I live next door, so if there's anything you want just knock."

She opened the door to room five and was briefly taken aback. Of course, it wasn't Norma's room any more but Mitsy didn't expect it to have changed so much. The room had been completely emptied, repainted in a soft cream colour while the walls were covered by an innocuous patterned wallpaper. The curtains were the same as when Norma had lived there but Mitsy could tell by the smell that they had been laundered to within an inch of their life and pressed with a steam iron so that they hung stiffly at the window.

"Here we are. I hope you will be comfortable. A bell sounds when it is mealtimes. I can knock for you today, if you like?"

Meena smiled her thanks and turned towards her wheelie suitcase, ready to make the room more personal.

Mitsy went straight into her room, closed the door and sat down on the bed. She realised that she had not posted Sky's letter but conceded that as it was the weekend it would not make much difference if she took it to the letter box tomorrow.

She could not resist sharing the news of this morning's happenings, so she wrote a message to Arthur:

> *Would you believe it, Arthur? All that dreadful rain has flooded the care home of some people living the other side of the city, so three of them have come to stay at Appledore House temporarily. One of them has moved into Norma's old room. Her name is Meena. She seems a bit shocked. I'm so glad we live on the top of a hill here.*
> *How are you? Anything exciting happening in your world? Mitsy x*

Mitsy always signed off all her emails with an X but she did worry sometimes if Arthur might misinterpret this. She knew he was fond of her, as she was of him, but she was one hundred per cent certain that it could only be as friends so far as she was concerned.

She had an unpleasant experience a while ago, when one of her husband's friends from long ago visited and made it clear that he was interested in a relationship with her. He had been the best man at their wedding but Peter had largely lost touch with him over the years. Mitsy concluded that the man was mainly after her money, which made her feel ghastly and let down. It also meant that she was wary of any male advances, however friendly.

Within minutes a reply came from Arthur:

> *Yes. What a shock it must have been. Two of them have moved in up here on the first floor.*

*They do seem rather distressed because they
had to leave in a hurry as the water was rising.*

*Not much happening here. Jackie is working
from home today and she phoned just for a chat.
I'll see you at lunchtime Mitsy.*

Mitsy was amused that their days were so punctuated by
mealtimes and in the absence of anything else to do she
called the cat over to her window, to give her a stroke.

In due course, as promised, she tapped on the door to
room five so that she could show Meena where to go for
lunch but after waiting a few minutes with no response she
set off alone.

Mitsy was rather distracted as she approached the dining
room, but she noticed out of the corner of her eye that the
oil painting in the hallway was missing. This was the one
that had been created by the Polish artist.

In the dining room, Maggie was waiting to address
everyone who was there:

"Hello everyone. I just wanted to let you know that we
have three guests staying with us at Appledore House for a
short while. As you no doubt know, the torrential rain we
have experienced locally and across the country has caused
some serious flooding. Meena, Judy and Charlotte were
unfortunately affected and along with several of their
friends they have had to leave Grove Park Care Home while
the waters recede and their rooms are dried out and
redecorated. So, where is Meena?"

Meena waved her hand and everyone called out hello.

"And Judy?" again a friendly chorus of hellos.

"And Charlotte, who prefers to be called Charley."

The assembled group said their hellos to Charley then
Maggie signalled to the staff that they could begin to serve
the lunch.

Mitsy had noticed several weeks earlier that their meals were becoming less imaginative and the ingredients seemed to be of poorer quality than before. Today's lunch was no exception. A serving plate with small slices of quiche was placed in the middle of the table, along with a salad as accompaniment.

Billy turned to head back to the kitchen but Mitsy was too quick for him. "I say Billy, where are the tomatoes and cucumber to go in this salad?" she asked.

Billy looked a bit uncomfortable, as if he was not sure if he was supposed to answer. He always found Mitsy a little intimidating but he did not dare ignore her. "Oh, I think the order was a bit short this week. We didn't get much lettuce either," he said, wondering if this was too much information.

Mitsy turned to Arthur who was already tucking into his food, so she decided it wasn't worth making a fuss.

She noticed that the three new people (it's probably best not to refer to them as 'refugees' she said to herself) were sitting together, which was understandable after their frightening experience escaping from the flood waters.

Much later, after lunch was finished and the tea and coffee cups had been cleared away, Mitsy asked Arthur if he had any plans for the afternoon.

"No. Well, maybe I will settle down with a book. I feel like a lazy read this afternoon. How about you?"

"That's a good idea Arthur. It's probably for the best in this ghastly weather," she said, glancing at the window where it was evident that the heavy rain and blustery winds had not eased up yet.

Mitsy could not remember if she had anything worth reading but she thought if the rain held off for a while, she could go to the post office where a good selection of newspapers would be available.

The rain did not abate. If anything, it seemed to be getting worse. Puss was still sitting outside of Mitsy's window.

"Shhh," said Mitsy to the cat, "if you want to come in you will have to be very quiet."

Of course, Puss was quiet in any case but she seemed to understand what Mitsy was saying and when the window was opened just enough for her to creep indoors, she did so with alacrity.

Mitsy sat in her comfortable chair, Puss purring gently in her lap, for a long while. It was perhaps one of the most relaxing afternoons that Mitsy had spent in recent times. It gave her a chance to reflect on life and all that had happened this year.

12

Troubled Times

It was always a bonus when the weather cleared up on a Wednesday so that Mitsy and Arthur could resume their weekly trip to the Stansfield Arms. Walking over together gave them a breath of fresh air, some modest exercise, and on this occasion, an opportunity to talk about Pete and Jackie's wedding. Arthur had brought with him a small photograph album which the newly-weds had sent him. Apart from showing the pictures to Mitsy, he knew that the pub staff would be pleased to see them too.

"We will be toasting their health and future happiness here, soon," said Arthur to the pub landlady as she took their order, "as soon as that son of Mitsy's can get a space in his busy work diary!"

Sitting in their usual corner, Mickey the new puppy dashed over to see them and nearly caused an accident with the drinks. Once the wedding photos had been admired and Mickey was removed to a safe place, they were able to relax.

"Arthur, can I ask you something?"

"Of course, my dear friend."

"Have you noticed how the meals at Appledore House have deteriorated recently?"

Arthur paused, reflected for a moment, then replied, "Well, yes, now you mention it I have. There isn't as much food on each plate and the quality is not what it was. I presume that the staff are having more difficulty sourcing ingredients than they used to. It's no secret from what I see on the news that there are shortages of fruit and vegetables. They were also saying that olive oil and toilet rolls were in short supply too."

"That's what I thought. The trouble is, they've also increased our monthly payments."

"I know. That's because electricity has gone up in price a great deal everywhere. The government was supposed to be helping people out over that but the letter we got from Mr Longhope said that it didn't apply to care homes so they had to increase our payments. I'm not sure we can do anything about it, as everyone is suffering at the moment.

"Yes, that's what I thought Arthur. The thing is, most of us who live at Appledore House are relatively protected from these troubles, but I think there must be lots of people who don't know how they are going to cope."

"Well, I think that's right. It must be very worrying if you have a family to feed or if you live in rented accommodation that the landlord plans to sell."

Mitsy and Arthur sat pondering these troublesome times before Mitsy changed the subject. Somehow Arthur felt he had not heard the last of this topic. Maybe Mitsy had an idea to help people?

"I must tell you something naughty," she giggled. "You know that beautiful black cat that wanders round the garden?"

"Mmm."

"Well, she keeps coming to see me."

"What's wrong with that?"

"Well, she comes in the window of my room, sits on my chair or even on my lap. She's really lovely, but I don't think I should be allowing her in, she must belong to someone."

"Oh, I don't think that would matter. Her owners probably think she's out hunting or something."

Mitsy was going to confess that Puss stayed overnight with her most nights but decided she had said enough, so she stopped. In any case, their lunch had arrived so they concentrated on enjoying that.

"Do you have any idea when Pete and Jackie might be able to visit us?" asked Arthur. "It's just a bit embarrassing as I've cancelled our dinner for four here twice!"

"No. I'm afraid not, Arthur. He seems to be very busy with something important at the moment. I will send him an email this afternoon."

It was Arthur's turn to pay (they took it in turns so that their lunch outings were fair) and he had thought he could re-arrange the family get-together while he was paying at the bar.

"Right then, Mitsy. I think we had better be heading back before the next downpour. I don't like this summer weather, do you?"

They managed to dodge the showers and within twenty minutes were ringing the door bell at Appledore House. Jo opened the door for them as there seemed to be a bit of a commotion going on, with Tracey appearing to direct some people up the stairs. Tracey had been one of the staff who had kindly stayed at Appledore House during the first lockdown and she was well-liked by all the residents.

Arthur nodded to Mitsy, "Well, thank you for your company this lunchtime Mitsy and I'll see you later."

Mitsy headed along the ground floor corridor towards her room, noticing as she went that the impressionist painting by the Polish artist was still missing.

By the time she opened the door to her room, she could hear her phone ringing.

It was Kate. "Oh Mitsy, I'm so glad I've got hold of you. One of those new people has just been diagnosed with covid. No one has told us anything yet but I thought it might be best if you don't have any contact with that Meena next door to you."

Mitsy thanked Kate for the alert and, realising that the unfortunate person was living upstairs, she immediately phoned Arthur to pass on the news to him.

By mid-afternoon the word had gone round to virtually everyone. Just to be careful, Maggie had decided that they would re-instate an in-house lockdown and she had personally called into every room, wearing a face mask, plastic apron and disinfecting every door knob. All the residents were told that dinner would be eaten alone in their rooms.

Anyone looking at Mitsy could see she was crestfallen. They had barely got used to the new normal. She concluded that there was no way that Pete and Jackie should plan to visit for the time being, so her email to Pete was clear on that point. She didn't know if Jackie was in London or Dublin so she cc'd Jackie and Arthur, just so everyone got the same information.

While she waited for dinner to be delivered, she poured herself a glass of ginger wine to cheer herself up.

'Would you believe it?! We've had floods, fire, famine and now pestilence!!' she grumbled to herself. Of course, the flooded care home did not directly affect her, although Elaine's car fire was frightening enough. Food shortages did not yet constitute a famine and a recurrence of covid was a nuisance but she hoped it would not spread around the home.

13

The White Lady

Mitsy was disappointed that it had been necessary to lockdown again.

Back when Pete suggested that she might be happier living in residential care rather than staying in the family home in Harrogate, she thought it might be preferable to feeling lonely on her own and with nothing to do except housework and gardening. Overall, she was in quite good health for her age but shopping, lifting, cleaning, weeding, ironing etc all took their toll and it was a great relief when so many of the daily chores were taken away from her.

Of course, it was not cheap to live at Appledore House but she and Pete had done their sums and calculated that the money raised from selling the family home would provide for a good number of years in residential care. They did joke that Pete would have to chip in, if she lived beyond her 100th birthday. Much as she looked forward to receiving a telegram from the Queen, Mitsy was sure that King Charles would continue the custom, if he was still around to do so!

Looking back over the time that Mitsy had lived at Appledore House, she was amazed at how easily she had kept herself fit, active and happy. She had flown, on her own, to Dublin to stay with Pete and that trip had included some ancestry research, some clothes shopping, and an outing to the races.

She often went for a short walk locally on her own to enjoy the fresh air, the green grass, some wild flowers and the trees. Occasionally she had the company of a friend. These outings were much more pleasurable than going to the paper shop or post office. She enjoyed the garden of Appledore House to walk around too, except for the time she accidentally got locked into the air-raid shelter.

The staff of Appledore House, before the pandemic, organised regular day trips and Mitsy had taken full advantage of these. There were also courses to attend, such as flower arranging and craft workshops.

Mitsy's own attempts at oil painting would probably be described as chaotic by those who preferred representational art. She did, however, recognise that some people such as her neighbour Raymond, had a real talent for drawing from life. She even sat for him once and was impressed by his skills.

And so, being locked down again presented Mitsy with the challenge to amuse her self as well as possible. Of course, she had already written her book entitled *Violet's Story* but she was not in the mood for repeating that experience as it requires detailed research and the effort of writing every day is laborious. She enjoyed reading but realised that she had read everything on her bookshelf as well as several eBooks that she had previously downloaded.

Mitsy was not enjoying being shut down again. She picked up the phone to talk to Arthur, since they could not go out for their weekly pub lunch outing. Then she thought better of it. Arthur probably would not appreciate an interruption to whatever he was doing, she thought.

She had been spending an increasing amount of time watching various antiques programmes on the television. The Antiques Roadshow, Bargain Hunt, Salvage Hunters, The Repair Shop, Flog It! The Bidding Room and Antiques Road Trip were firm favourites. She realised that not all the items they showcased were antiques, some were reproductions and others were curios. It was interesting though and she was amused to notice that some of the china she had taken to the charity shop before she moved to Appledore House had probably been of some significant value. Each time something like the items at Appledore House came up on a TV programme, she got out her notebook and jotted down dates, makers, and value. This kept her entertained for hours. Probably because the weather had been so dreadful, she had been forced to stay indoors and so was able to indulge this latest project.

Under different circumstances, she was not much of a television watcher, preferring to spend her time out of doors or browsing the local shops. During the earlier lockdown Mitsy and her friends had all got used to ordering things online. In fact, at one stage because Mitsy was good at such things on the internet, she was besieged by fellow residents asking her to order things for them. Once Maggie realised that this was becoming a burden to Mitsy, she set up some alternative arrangements by offering a part-time job to a school leaver.

Now that they were confined to their rooms, the television was appreciated again.

The residents were told that Judy, who was one of the three women staying at Appledore House temporarily because their care home had been flooded, was the unfortunate soul to have caught covid. The word went round that she was not dreadfully ill, but was being kept isolated so that the virus would not spread. It was hoped that Judy, along with all the other residents, would be less seriously affected because they had all had a full set of vaccinations as well as boosters.

Much of this information was conveyed by Joyce when she came round with the evening medication. All the staff were wearing PPE again and had quickly adjusted to their revised routine of delivering meals outside people's doors, waiting for a couple of hours, and then collecting the dirty plates to be washed up.

"Joyce, do you know why that oil painting that was hanging just inside the front door has been moved?" asked Mitsy. Joyce was not aware of this painting and to be honest it did not really feature in her list of daily priorities but she promised to find out for Mitsy. Mitsy realised that this could take several days.

Meanwhile, Puss had decided that she would be comfortable staying with Mitsy every night. She often appeared outside the bedroom window just when Mitsy finished her dinner and was taking her tray to be collected later from outside her door.

'I know it's silly of me, but I do enjoy your company Puss. If we don't tell anyone, I'm happy for you to sleep at the end of my bed every night. I love to hear your purr when I'm not asleep.'

Mitsy had a lifelong difficulty in sleeping. She did not like to describe herself as an insomniac because that sounded like there was something wrong with her. It was merely that she did not sleep the whole night through. She was quite excited to discover recently that in medieval times it was natural for everyone to have two sleeps. Recent research showed that this habit of biphasic sleep was found in many cultures around the world. It was speculated that the custom disappeared with the advent of electric lighting. Whatever the case, Mitsy usually went to bed around nine or ten at night, slept until one o'clock, spent a couple of hours reading or just awake, before returning to the land of nod.

Before the pandemic, Mitsy sometimes visited the small room behind the kitchen, to see whichever member of staff was on night duty, where she cadged a cup of tea. No one really minded as Mitsy was pleasant company.

These night-time awakenings were often the time when Mitsy saw the person she called the White Lady. After a while, she reached the conclusion that she was a young woman called Violet who became a nurse when Appledore

House became a hospital for wounded soldiers during the First World War. Arthur had carried out research on the former use of Appledore House and Mitsy had, with some imaginative embellishments, turned this information into a novel called **Violet's Story**. At the time that Mitsy's book was published everyone was quite proud of their fledgling author, although a few people were not so impressed to think that a ghost inhabited the care home.

The next evening, Joyce tapped on Mitsy's door to distribute her medication. There was little improvement in Judy's health so the lockdown continued.

"Good evening Mitsy. Here's your evening tablets. How are you feeling?"

Mitsy confirmed that she was quite well.

"I remembered to ask about that oil painting. Maggie said that it had gone away to be cleaned. I think she said that the valuers advised that it would be worth more like that."

Mitsy thanked Joyce but still felt rather confused. Who were the valuers? Why were things being valued? Why were they sneaking around the house – rather than being open about their purpose - looking at paintings and antiques?

A small part of the answer came sooner than expected. Mitsy's friend Kate rang for a chat. Kate lived upstairs and she was as bored as everyone else with the imposed lockdown, although of course she hoped that Judy would recover soon.

During their conversation, Kate mentioned Mrs Podsiadlo. "Did you know that Mrs P has been quite ill?" she asked Mitsy.

"Oh dear no. Is it the dementia or something else?"

"Well apparently, she had a minor stroke. She has been in hospital but is back in her care home now. Mr Longhope has had to deal with some of the legal implications."

"I didn't know there were any legal implications, Kate. How do you know all this?"

"A friend of mine is in the same care home as Mrs P. so she tells me things, on the days when she's not confused. She said that Mrs P still owns Appledore House."

"I don't think that can be right Kate," said Mitsy.

"Well Mr Longhope bought the business in exchange for giving Mrs P lifetime accommodation in one of his care homes that specialises in dementia care."

"Hmm. I see. I did know that. But I just thought the house was included in it."

"It seems not. So, they are trying to sort out what would happen to the house if/ when she dies. A new will is being drawn up."

"Well, I jolly well hope they get it all sorted. It makes me feel quite vulnerable in case Appledore House has to be sold. Mind you, that probably explains why the antiques are being valued."

Kate was not aware of anything to do with the antiques, but Mitsy just gave her the barest outline as she wanted to think it all through herself. She trusted Kate absolutely, but Mitsy was also aware how easily gossip can spread like wildfire.

They finished their conversation with Mitsy promising Kate that they would go for a walk together as soon as they were allowed outside again.

Not surprisingly, much of this was mulled over all evening and Mitsy would have found it quite difficult to go off to sleep, were it not for the gentle purr of Puss who seemed to know when she was troubled. Curled up by Mitsy's feet, she was a warm and comforting presence.

When Mitsy did wake, it was pitch dark and she rightly guessed it was the middle of the night. However, over by the window was a white glow which soon revealed itself to be the White Lady or Violet, as Mitsy was happy to call her.

"Oh. Hello Violet. You haven't visited me for such a long time that I assumed you had gone away"

She never heard any response from Violet but she was quite happy to speak softly to her. Mitsy was probably correct in observing previously that Violet seemed to appear when she was worried about something.

From a quick glance at her alarm Mitsy could see that it was after one o'clock. She rarely used the alarm to wake up but as it had a phosphorescent dial this was handy in the night. She noticed that the air was quite cold. 'That's probably because of the rain' she said to herself. Then she noticed something else, or to be more precise she noticed its absence. Where was Puss? The door was locked and the window closed so she could not have got out. How curious!

Looking over at Violet again, she could see that the ghostly figure was busy. It was almost as if she was bending down at regular intervals to look at something as she walked around the room. Mitsy suddenly realised that it was as if she was back during the war carrying out her hospital duties, calling at every bed to check on the patients. When the ghostly figure reached the door, she nodded as if to say 'that's all OK' then she bent down low. Mitsy watched, spellbound. In front of her eyes, Violet faded into the dark and at the exact same time, Puss leapt up on Mitsy's bed purring loudly.

Mitsy reached down towards Puss and gave her a gentle stroke. Puss was happy and she curled up in her usual place to go to sleep. Mitsy felt quite calm and before her busy mind could question what she had seen, she fell into a calm and deep sleep.

14

Live Long, Live Well

Eventually, all the residents of Appledore House were given a clean bill of health. Judy's covid tests were clear and the care home where Judy, Meena and Charlotte came from was dried out, dehumidified, aired, and redecorated so that the three of them could return. Everyone breathed a sigh of relief that they could go back to normal.

It seemed that while the latest local lockdown was in place, the staff had carried out a thorough Spring clean in all the common rooms. There was a strong smell of lavender polish and all the wood surfaces gleamed. Mitsy noticed that all of the oil paintings and antique ceramics had been removed and so she assumed that was all part of the clean-up.

She and Arthur were planning to resume their weekly trip to the Standsfield Arms; they had missed their lunchtime outings, chatting to the staff and making a fuss of Mickey. They also hoped to book a table for four for the coming Saturday as, at last, it seemed they could conclude their wedding celebrations with Jackie and Pete.

She was just opening her wardrobe and sighing that she had nothing new to wear when there was a firm but gentle knock on the door. Mitsy, ever polite, walked to the door to see who was there.

"Oh, hello Maggie. Do come in," she said to the kind and hard working head of Appledore House. Some people called her Matron but she did not really like the title and

Mitsy was careful to address her by name, unless Mr Longhope was around and, in that case, she referred to her as Mrs Baxter.

"Good morning Mitsy," she said as she sat down opposite her favourite resident. Of course, they were not supposed to have favourites, but it happened anyway.

"I've got some good news and some sad news, Mitsy," she said. Without pausing for a reaction, she launched straight away into the news she had to share. Maggie had to call in to speak to each resident and she was starting with Mitsy, knowing that this would offer a rehearsal for a difficult conversation with some people.

"First, the sad news. I'm sorry to say that Mrs Podsiadlo passed away last night. I'm sure you were aware that she had not been well for quite a while. Mr Longhope's staff were very fond of her and supported her right to the end. Mrs P was very well thought of when she and her husband ran Appledore House and we will be thinking about how we can honour her memory."

Maggie paused for breath, just long enough for Mitsy to offer her condolences and reminisce how kind she and Antoni had been to her when she first moved into Appledore House.

"Now, I know that some rumours have been flying around about our home here so I just wanted to reassure you all that the ownership of the building is being sorted out and there is nothing to worry about."

Again, Mitsy was given just long enough to say that she was reassured to hear this news and was not concerned about the future.

At this point, Maggie stood up to leave when she suddenly turned round and sat down again.

"I almost forgot! I have some good news, I think, just for you."

Mitsy looked puzzled.

"Do you remember a young girl called Beth Mackenzie?"

"The name is a little familiar but I cannot think where from. Did she work here?"

"No. If I remember rightly," said Maggie, "when she was at school, she wrote to you about *Violet's Story* because she thought she could be distantly related to the Doughty family and she wanted to know more about the research you had done about Appledore House and the Doughty family during the war."

"Oh yes. I remember now. Someone had shown her the article that dreadful journalist had written about me and she got in touch. We wrote to each other for a while but I've since lost touch."

"Well, she's written to me on behalf of her employer and I received a formal request from her to ask if she could contact you. It seems she is working for a charity and they have plans to write a guide for older people, to help them think through the implications of moving into a care home. The charity is a national one, called Live Long, Live Well."

"Oh. That sounds interesting and I'd be happy to help her. She was at school in the Highlands when we were in touch before. We could talk on the phone or maybe she would be willing to travel down here."

"Fine. Leave it with me Mitsy and I will see what I can organise." Maggie headed once more for the door, aware that these conversations would take all morning.

Outside stood Val, with a mug of coffee made just how Mitsy liked it.

Mitsy sipped her hot drink and reflected on the conversation. It would be lovely to meet Beth if that were possible and if not, a conversation on the phone would be enjoyable. It was good to think that Beth had started work with a charity for older people. Mitsy thought of several national charities relating to older people but she had not heard of Live Long, Live Well.

She was quite keen to help with the task of writing a guide for people in a similar position to herself, although she realised that probably nothing would come of it for weeks or months.

Mitsy remembered that when she and Pete discussed whether she should move into a care home, they had written a big list of pro's and con's. 'I wonder if I kept that list?' she asked herself before delving into the desk drawer in the hope that she would find it.

It was there, and Mitsy was quite amused to see what helped to sway her decision in the end was the fact that her cat had just died. She remembered saying to Pete that she was lonely now she was all alone in the house. She put the crumpled notes back in the desk drawer so that she could find them easily when, or if, Beth visited.

After lunch, Mitsy and Kate sat outside on one of the garden benches. It had not rained that morning so the bench was dry and the air was warm.

Kate wordlessly offered Mitsy an extra strong mint.

"Thank you, Kate. I haven't had any sweets for ages."

Kate smiled. "Do you remember going to the sweet shop when you were little?" she asked.

"I do. I wasn't allowed to go very often because mum thought we would lose our teeth if we had too many sweeties!"

"My mum used to say to me 'now, Caitlin, you can only spend tuppence today'."

"Hehe. I'd forgotten about those old pennies. They were so big compared to today's tiny decimal coins. You could get four black jacks for a penny."

"And four fruit salads for a penny too. Mind you, I preferred the sherbet fountain with the liquorish straw to suck through; I invariably coughed and choked on it even thought I loved it."

"My favourites were 'shrimps' and 'flying saucers'," said Mitsy.

"Hmm. It's so different for young people today. Ours was such an innocent time, in some ways. I know we had just got through the war and anything sweet, after rationing, was truly a treat. These days, children are terrified they are going to put on weight, stressed that they are not wearing or doing what the latest influencer suggests and frightened that something horrible will happen to them."

"I suppose so," said Mitsy "they certainly don't have the freedom to wander the streets playing these days."

"My niece's kids seem to spend all their time on their phones, rather than talking to each other."

"My Pete was into all sorts of things as a teenager. He was obsessive about skateboarding and had to wear all the 'accepted' brands of tee-shirts, sweatshirts, and footwear, none of which was cheap. Still, he was outdoors with his mates so I suppose that was good."

"Well, every generation has its craze or fashion. I believe the term 'teenage' was coined in our era."

Kate and Mitsy smiled at these reminiscences and would probably have continued if Raymond had not been spotted strolling across the grass to them.

"How are you two ladies?" he asked. Then he smiled, "is that OK to say these days or will you be offended? I don't want to be cancelled by my favourite neighbours!"

They smiled and assured Raymond that the term ladies would be fine.

"In fact, Raymond, we were just saying how hard it is for young people these days. We've been reminiscing about being allowed to buy sweeties."

"Have you ever been to Beamish? It's an open-air museum with original buildings from the past including a sweet shop and a Victorian classroom and the people who run it dress up in the costume of the time."

"Oh, that sounds interesting Raymond, perhaps we could ask for an outing there?"

"That's an idea," said Kate and Raymond together. They laughed. "Well, next time I'm talking to Maggie I will ask, if you like?" said Mitsy.

15

Not As Easy As You Think

Mitsy was quietly enjoying her toast and marmalade when she became aware of an uncomfortable atmosphere at the far end of the breakfast table. There wasn't anything she could put her finger on, just an awareness that the easy, gentle chatter had come to an abrupt halt.

After the residents had all finished, Billy came in to clear the table and Mitsy waited until Eva stood up to leave. "Eva, may I have a word?" said Mitsy and the pair wandered off slowly together towards Mitsy's room.

"Is everything OK?" she asked

"Well, sort of," said Eva. Mitsy waited until her friend was ready to say more. Eva was still quite new at Appledore House and maybe there had been a minor misunderstanding.

Inside room six, Mitsy discreetly brushed off the chair in case there was evidence that Puss had been sleeping there overnight and gestured to Eva.

"Well, its funny Mitsy. I thought everyone here was kind and friendly but I'm beginning to have my doubts about Mariam."

Mitsy frowned and nodded, to encourage Eva to say more.

"Someone said they liked my cardigan and I said thank you and then mentioned that it was one of my 'colours'. Mariam asked what I meant and so I explained about the colours session we went to. Mariam got angry because she had wanted to go to that but no one had told her when it was, so she missed it. I thought it would be helpful to say that there would be another one soon as Julie said she would come back for a session on style. Unfortunately, that seemed to annoy Mariam even more and she started to go on about not needing anyone to tell her what clothes suited her. I thought it best to change the subject so I mentioned the weather forecast which is looking quite good for today. Mariam then said 'oh do shut up Eva, we are trying to eat our breakfast.' So, I stopped talking and so did everyone else."

"Ahh. I wondered why it suddenly went quiet," said Mitsy.

"I'm really not sure why I seemed to annoy her," said Eva, verging on tears.

"Now, don't you worry about her. I've noticed that Mariam can be quite rude. To be honest, she reminds me a bit of my sister. Sky can pick a fight with anyone about anything and she is always convinced that she is in the right. Perhaps Mariam got out of the wrong side of the bed!"

Once Eva seemed calmer, Mitsy suggested she was thinking of going to the post office, if Eva wanted to accompany her on a short walk. Eva said she had other things to do, so they went their separate ways.

On her way out of Appledore House en route to the post office, Mitsy heard raised voices and was shocked to see Mariam red-faced and appearing to stamp her foot in conversation with Tessa, who had recently started work as a cleaner.

Mitsy was unsure whether to intervene but concluded that would be interfering.

The post office was busy when she got there so she joined the queue which was moving quite slowly. At least there were plenty of things to look at on the displays of cards, packets of sweets and even – heaven forbid – some Christmas decorations.

The queue moved up slowly and when the door opened Mitsy realised that Mariam had just come in. She smiled and decided it might be best not to engage her in conversation.

Mariam was definitely not in a good mood and it appeared that she had decided to involve Mitsy in whatever was troubling her.

"That Eva drives me round the bend," she said, raising her voice so that everyone in the queue could hear, as well as the two post office staff who were clearly working as fast as they could to deal with the queue waiting at the counters.

"Oh, that is a shame. I think she is just starting to settle in. I remember how uncomfortable I was in my first few weeks at Appledore House," said Mitsy, hoping to calm things down.

"Well, that's her problem. She shouldn't annoy other people just because of that."

Mitsy concluded that any further conversation with Mariam was not going to be pleasant today, so she turned towards the post office counter and hoped sincerely that she would be served soon.

Fortunately, the queue moved up quite quickly and so Mitsy spent the next couple of minutes appearing to rummage in her handbag to look for something until she was served.

Once her postage stamps were purchased, she headed straight for the door and walked back home as quickly as she could go, without actually breaking into a run.

Indoors, there were two letters addressed to herself on the sideboard which she scooped into her handbag to read later.

At that moment Tessa came out of Maggie's room, apparently in tears. Mitsy, always kind and thoughtful, asked if she was alright.

"Not really," said Tessa, wiping her eyes.

"Come and sit here for a minute," suggested Mitsy, pointing to a bench seat. "What's happened?"

"Well, I seem to have really annoyed one of the residents and she has complained about me to Mrs Baxter. I was just starting to enjoy working here but I'm afraid I will get the sack."

"Oh, I don't know. Maggie is generally very reasonable and I'm sure you did not mean to upset anyone. We older people can get a bit crotchety, you know."

Tessa sniffed, wiped her eyes, and smiled at Mitsy. "Thank you very much. I'd better get on with dusting the dining room."

Mitsy had guessed it was Mariam who was involved and as she didn't want to cross her path once she got in from the post office, she immediately headed for her own room.

It was good to receive a letter from Sky, which was – for once – not too grumpy. It seemed that Jim was feeling better and was recovering from covid and Sky was also happy to congratulate Pete and Jackie on their marriage, without sounding as if she wished she had been invited.

The other letter was from Jackie. It was a pretty notelet and the contents added to Mitsy's good opinion of her. Jackie had realised that today was the anniversary of Mitsy's husband Peter's death. Probably Pete had told her. She had just sent a few words saying that she was thinking of Mitsy today. What a thoughtful young woman her son's new wife was!

Mitsy was rather troubled to think that she had not remembered the date herself but then she was much more likely to think of Peter on their wedding anniversary and his birthday.

Just as Mitsy was wondering how she might fill her morning after her trip to the post office, there was a knock at the door.

"Come in, Kate."

Kate had a strange expression of her face that Mitsy was not able to fathom.

"Hello Mitsy. How are you?"

"I'm fine thank you," she replied. "I must tell you what has just happened to me," she said, barely pausing for breath.

"I was going to the sideboard in the hall, you know, the one by the front door, to see if there was any mail. There was just one letter from an old school friend that I keep in touch with. I opened it to start reading it, when that Mariam came in the door. Do you know, Mitsy, she pushed past me – shoving me to one side with her hands – and shouted at me."

"Fortunately, I didn't fall over but I was very wobbly. She said: 'for goodness sake get out of my way woman!!' I was so shocked I couldn't say anything. It was really unpleasant."

Mitsy hugged her friend. "Wow, that's horrible Kate."

"I don't think I was in her way, she just wanted to be nasty."

"Well, she seems to have been very upset with several people today. I don't know what's wrong with her. I think we'd all better keep a low profile until she's got over it."

Kate and Mitsy chatted for a few minutes and when Kate returned to her room Mitsy said, "Take care!"

It wasn't until nearly lunchtime that Mitsy had an idea. She decided to go a few minutes early for lunch and tapped gently on Maggie's door, which was next to the dining room.

"Excuse me, Maggie. May I have a quick word?"

"Of course, Mitsy, what can I do for you?"

Maggie was used to residents calling into her room for a chat or to complain about something. Thankfully the latter was not common but she saw it as a key part of her role in managing Appledore House to keep abreast of anything the residents were concerned about.

"You may, perhaps, be aware that one of the residents seems to be rather 'fractious' today."

Mitsy wasn't quite sure if that was the correct word but as Maggie didn't question it, she carried on.

"She has shouted at other residents and a member of staff and she also tried to start a row with me in the post office." Mitsy took a deep breath.

"I am not complaining. I just remember many years ago that one of my neighbours, when I lived in Harrogate, went through a phase of being angry for no obvious reason. Eventually they discovered that she had undiagnosed diabetes. Apparently, it's a known phenomenon."

Maggie nodded and smiled. "I know who you are referring to Mitsy and that thought had already briefly crossed my mind. Thank you for drawing my attention to it. I had thought it was just a one-off but if she has been bad tempered with several people, we need to do something about it, especially if a pattern is emerging. Leave it with me and I will see what we can do."

Maggie smiled again at Mitsy. She really wasn't nosey; it was just that she had a lively mind that was always seeking to make sense of things. Maggie made a note on some paper on her desk, to remind herself to talk to the GP practice and see if they could do a fasting blood test for Mariam, if she was willing. That last part would be difficult. Everyone thought that running care home was a simple matter of keeping a group of kindly old women and men warm, safe, clean and fed. She often said to her friends 'ah, its not as easy as you think' but they didn't believe her.

16

The Plot Thickens

Appledore House returned to its somewhat more relaxed way of life after the departure of Judy, Meena and Charlotte; this was helped by everyone, including the staff, becoming reasonably relaxed that covid had again been excluded from their midst.

Mitsy and Arthur resumed their Wednesday lunchtimes at the Standsfield Arms. Finally, Jackie and Pete were able to visit their parents and a pleasant celebratory lunch was also held in the pub, even though their wedding had been a few months earlier.

Kate and Mitsy enjoyed a few gentle walks when the weather was suitable. It had been inordinately wet and often the dinner table discussion centred around climate change, its impact and what the government really ought to do about it.

Elaine and Mitsy enjoyed their weekly coffee and chats too. Thankfully, Elaine's insurance payout had enabled her to buy a modest second-hand car to replace the one that went up in smoke. It was small and rather flimsy by comparison but at least she had the sense not to resort to pressure from Martin who was initially keen to move in with her. Elaine had heard little from her son Grant but her approach was to assume that 'no news is good news'.

Mitsy was happy that daily life had returned to normal, but she could not help wondering what had happened to the oil painting by the Polish artist, especially now the news of Mrs Podsiadlo's death was public knowledge.

The ceramic pieces she had admired also seemed to have disappeared and she was saddened that she did not have them to look at any more in the public rooms, just as she was learning about antiques from her study of the internet and TV programmes.

Joyce, who usually did the evening medication round, was on holiday so Anna took on this task. One evening Anna found that she had forgotten to bring one of Mitsy's night-time tablets and promised to call back once she had seen everyone else.

Around nine o'clock there was a gentle tap on the door. Anna was carrying a hot chocolate drink for Mitsy by way of an apology for missing her out earlier. She was about to end her shift but for once was not really in a hurry to get home so when Mitsy asked if she wanted to give her feet a rest for a few minutes she was happy to do so.

"Is there any news about the ownership of Appledore House?" she asked. Mitsy was of the view that if there was something worrying her it was always best to address the problem head on.

"Well, I think it is all sorted and Mr Longhope has bought the freehold of the property. You know how it is Mitsy, the solicitors always seem to find things to quibble over so I don't think it is official yet. I'm sure Maggie will tell us all once the paperwork is signed."

"Oh, that will be a relief," sighed Mitsy. "I suppose they will have to sort out the furniture and fixtures, not to mention the things that were valued by the antiques specialists."

"Hmm. I don't know anything about that?"

"Well, there's a valuable oil painting that used to hang by the front door and that has gone to be cleaned. Also, all sorts of other valuable china like Clarice Cliff and

Moorcroft. I think they were moved somewhere else when you all did the Spring clean, as none of them are here now."

Anna looked puzzled. "I'm not aware of things being moved. I can't even picture what you mean."

At this, Mitsy fetched her notebook and phone so she could show Anna the list of items that were originally in the house including those she had taken photos of.

They agreed that it was all rather a conundrum and Anna said that she would ask Maggie where the painting and other things had gone. With that, she left as she did need to go home now even though she liked chatting to Mitsy.

Puss had been waiting patiently outside Mitsy's window and as soon as Anna left, Mitsy could see the cat's face peering in expectantly. After a few minutes sitting on Mitsy's lap for a stroke and rather exuberant purring, she stepped down gently and arranged herself at the end of Mity's bed, ready for a good night's sleep.

Mitsy smiled. There wasn't anything that she wanted to see on the TV tonight so she gave in to Puss's unspoken request and turned in for the night too.

17

Beth

Mitsy had almost forgotten her conversation with Maggie about the request for help from Beth Mackenzie. It turned out that Maggie, with Mitsy's agreement, had passed on Mitsy's email address to Beth.

Beth wrote:

Dear Mrs Howard (may I call you Mitsy?)

You may remember that I got in touch with you a while ago for my school homework as I wanted to find out if the Doughty family, who originally owned Appledore House, were related to me. Thank you for your help then; with your support I was able to discover that Violet Doughty and her brother were in fact distantly related to our family and cousins to my great-grandfather.

I have since left school and I am working for Live Long, Live Well; this is a charitable organisation which provides services for older people. I have explained to your Matron that I am writing a guide which will help people as they think through the implications of moving into residential care.

*I remembered you and your helpful common sense, as well as your achievement in writing the novel **Violet's Story** and I wondered if you*

Of course, Mitsy had already understood much of this from Maggie so she wrote back immediately, confirming her willingness to help.

In due course she received the questions which were quite straightforward. She printed them off and made notes in the margin, in preparation for their phone call.

Later the same day, as she and Arthur strolled up to the Standsfield Arms for lunch, Mitsy mentioned her renewed contact with Beth as well as the reason for the planned phone call.

"Well, Mitsy. It's an interesting topic. For my own part I had never given any thought to moving into residential care while Ivy was alive. Even afterwards, although it was a massive adjustment, I was managing just fine living on my own – or so I thought. As you know, one day I tripped very badly on the pavement outside my house and ended up in hospital with cuts, bruises, and a broken arm. My daughters came to see me in hospital and both Jackie and Marie tried to convince me to move down to London to be nearer to them. But I didn't really think I'd fit in to London life at my age. Their main argument was 'what if it happens again?' I suppose for most people the decision to give up one's independence happens when there is a crisis."

Mitsy nodded silently. She found Arthur's comments useful and mentally tucked them away for her conversation with Beth.

"Yes. I suppose that's true. I didn't have a crisis but to be honest I just found I was exhausted all the time. It had become a juggling act trying to keep the house cleaned, the garden tidy and the shopping, washing and ironing etc. under control. When Pete suggested it to me, we thought about the benefits and I had to agree that no housework, no cooking and freedom from all those things I had to do for myself was appealing."

They smiled as they arrived at the pub and Mickey the new puppy, who had already grown quite big, came to greet them.

After lunch, they returned to the topic of conversation from earlier.

"What concerned you most about moving to Appledore House, Arthur?"

"I think I was worried about being closeted with a load of older people who were boring and infirm! Then I met you and I realised that the move gave me a chance to get to know different people that I wouldn't have been able to otherwise."

"Thank you! I shall take that as a compliment then," smiled Mitsy to her friend. "It was different for me," she said. "I was worried that we could not afford the fees. Then I was worried about communal living; maybe that was a bit like you. Most of all I didn't want to lose my independence."

"On the other hand, I was so tired all the time that I looked forward to someone else cleaning, cooking, washing and ironing, not to mention the relief I felt when I realised that I would not be stuck indoors because Appledore House has a lovely garden."

"Did you used to feel safe when you lived on your own?" asked Arthur.

"Yes. I did, most of the time. But every time there was an escaped prisoner or a horrible break-in or murder, I started to feel insecure. By contrast, I feel safe here, the carers are lovely and always kind and there's not much to worry about any more."

Arthur nodded and commented: "although some of those TV adverts drive me mad, I think there's something to be said for their oft-quoted 'peace of mind'!"

"You're so right, Arthur. We know that someone will look after us no matter what."

"Well, I'm not so sure about those of us who go wandering off into derelict buildings in the dead of night, or get themselves locked in unoccupied air-raid shelters!"

Mitsy laughed. She didn't mind Arthur teasing her because he meant well.

In fact, the next morning she began sharing some of this conversation with others over the breakfast table. It was interesting to discover what constituted peace of mind when they had each considered the potential benefits of moving into residential care. Family complications were often mentioned, such as not wanting to be a burden to others. Probably the most important factor in many people's choice was the fact that Appledore House felt "right" from the outset.

All this was very useful, as Mitsy was expecting a phone call from Beth later this morning.

Beth rang Mitsy on the dot of eleven o'clock, as proposed in her email. Mitsy was delighted to find that Beth was very much as she had imagined, sounding bright and cheerful with a soft Scottish accent.

"Now, I'd like to begin with a few thoughts from me, then we can go through your questions and my answers. Is that OK, Beth?" Mitsy was always one to take control; sometimes that was irritating to other people but it was well intended.

"That's great thank you, Mrs Howard."

"Oh, do call me Mitsy, everyone does. Right. These are my top ideas:

- find out the fees of your local residential care home and work out what is included and how you will pay. This needs to be funded for several years.

- research the local homes and check reviews, opinions, and recent reports by the CQC (Care Quality Commission).

- discuss with family or friends the pro's and con's of moving to a care home versus staying where you are.

- find out which homes have vacancies and arrange to visit, preferably with a friend or family member, taking with you a note of any questions you want to ask. Notice which home feels "right".

"That all sounds sensible," said Beth.

"Of course, this applies only to people who are reading your guide and thinking through whether they want to make the move. What I have discovered, from talking to my friends here, which of course is not a representative sample, is that most people go into residential care as a result of a crisis. So, I would suggest that you need to design your guide for those people too."

At this point Mitsy shared several examples about the many and varied fears that her friends had, before moving into a care home.

"My assumption is that you are not 'selling' care homes in your publication but trying to help people come to informed decisions."

"That's right Mitsy. I knew you would understand! I really wish that you were working for Live Long, Live Well; I'm afraid some of my colleagues are all too ready to believe everything that care home companies tell them."

"Well, I have lots of other ideas but I think we have to be careful not to frighten your readers."

Beth was quiet for a moment, then asked, "can you give me an example?"

Mitsy took a deep breath: " I did not do this myself, but I probably would now. People might want to check with Companies House, to make sure that the owners of a care home are financially viable. You can do this, for free, on line. It's because you don't want to move in and then the business goes bankrupt."

"Hmm. That makes sense, but it's rather sad," observed Beth.

"True. Let's go through your questions systematically now Beth, if you wish."

By the time they had completed this and Beth had carefully written down in long hand all the useful suggestions made by Mitsy, she was feeling exhausted.

"Wow. That's amazing, Mitsy. I think you have virtually written my guide for me. Can I suggest that we both have a rest now? I would like to get on with writing this up while it is all still fresh in my mind. When I've done that, may I send you the first draft?"

"Of course, Beth. I would very much like to see how it turns out."

"I will, of course, credit you as my professional adviser!"

Mitsy laughed. "I don't know about that Beth, but do let me know how you get on."

Mitsy was tired after her phone call with Beth. In fact, she may have dropped off to sleep for a while. She liked Beth and she was pleased to be able to help her.

18

Tête-à-tête with Gerald Longhope

One morning, Mitsy was relaxing in her rocking chair before going to breakfast, when there was a knock at her door. This was unusual, as she invariably knew in advance if a fellow resident was calling at this time.

She glanced across at the office chair in front of her desk, where Puss was sitting. She was fast asleep and it seemed a shame to move her, so Mitsy answered the door in the hope that the visitor was not planning to stay.

It was Maggie. "Hello Mitsy! I was just checking that you were up and dressed. I know you are usually an early riser but as Mr Longhope wanted to talk to you, I thought it best to be sure you were ready to receive an unexpected guest."

Mitsy felt like asking what Mr Longhope wanted at this time of the morning, but it seemed rather rude, so she smiled and indicated that she was ready for anyone.

"I will just go and fetch him," said Maggie.

This gave Mitsy just enough time to open her window, scoop up Puss and encourage her to sit on the boxes outside the window. Puss managed a rather feeble miaow of displeasure; she got away with staying in Mitsy's room enough to know that she would not have been ejected unless it was necessary.

Mitsy wondered where Puss really lived as she spent a great deal of her time lurking around in the garden at Appledore House during the day and with Mitsy at night.

She did not seem to be feral as she was always clean and appeared well-fed.

Mitsy glanced in the bathroom mirror. She had recently been to the hairdressers so her hair was neat and, she noticed, quite shiny.

A gentle knock at her door announced Gerald Longhope and Mitsy opened the door. Before she could say hello or react in any way a very large bouquet of colourful summer flowers was thrust towards her.

"Oh. Oh. It's not my birthday, you know," she said. "Do come in, Mr Longhope. Sit down," she gestured to the spare chair.

"Good morning, Mitsy. I'm sure you know me well enough to call me Gerald," he said. "I know it's not your birthday yet. This is to say thank you."

Mitsy looked puzzled. "Whatever for?" she replied, thinking as she said it that she sounded impolite. "But thank you very much!"

She took the flowers into her bathroom, placed them in the wash basin and ran some cold water over the stems.

As she sat down on her rocking chair, facing Mr Longhope, he began to explain.

"Do you remember asking Maggie if she knew what had happened to the oil painting that was hanging in the hall?"

"Yes, I do."

"And you very helpfully kept a note, and photos, of many of the valuable items that subsequently went missing?"

"Yes."

"Well, at last the mystery has been uncovered. It seems that the man and woman who came to the house under the pretext of carrying out a valuation of our antiques were, in fact, running a fraudulent scheme. Maggie thought that I had booked them, and I thought she had booked them. When you first saw these people, they were 'casing the joint' – I think that is what it is called."

Mitsy looked shocked and shook her head in disbelief that everyone had been so easily fooled.

"Once you had pointed out to Anna that things were going missing, as well as giving her your notes and photos, she told Maggie and we immediately involved the police. To give them their due, the police were highly efficient and they were able to check with all the local auction houses to see if anyone could recognise these stolen goods. The Four Winds Auction House came up trumps and were able to stop the items from being sold."

"Oh, my goodness. Fancy that!" grinned Mitsy, rather enjoying the story.

"Now, we have not got the Polish artist's oil painting or any of the china pieces back yet, but we have every hope of doing so. The police think it unlikely that they will track the couple down, although I suppose if they move on to carry out this scam in other homes around the area, the police will be on the alert."

Gerald smiled at Mitsy. "It does mean that we shall have to set up some new arrangements for all visitors to the building. I guess we have got a bit lax over opening the door to anyone who says they are family or friends of our residents, especially after the covid regulations were relaxed."

He paused for breath while Mitsy nodded in agreement. "Of course, it's not just Appledore House, but all our homes will need to tighten up their systems."

At last, Mitsy was able to get a word in edgeways: "I am pleased I was able to help but I do hope you don't think I'm being nosey, Gerald. It's just that I notice things and I get pleasure from learning something new. Once I had noticed how many antiques we had here, I wanted to know more about them. So I've been watching all those antique programmes on the TV as well as making good use of the internet."

"Far from it, Mitsy. You are an asset to Appledore House and I am very grateful that you noticed that something out of the ordinary was taking place. Your research was critical and it provided exactly the evidence that was needed. You know, maybe we have teased you a little in the past for allowing your curiosity full rein but I for one think that it is an admirable trait, especially in an older person who could be forgiven for losing interest in the world around them."

He took a deep breath after this speech, and smiled broadly. "So, the flowers are just our way of saying thank you for being you!"

He stood up and was heading for the door when Misty asked, "Is this public information or shall I keep it to myself for now?"

"I think it would be wise to keep this under wraps. I suppose there is a possibility that the thieves have a connection to either residents or a member of staff, so we should wait until the police tell us that the case is closed."

Misty closed the door quietly behind Mr Longhope and started to arrange the flowers. There were so many in the bouquet that they would easily fill two vases. She checked her watch and realised that it was still over fifteen minutes until breakfast time.

Standing at the window, she could see the garden that Greg and Alan tended so carefully, Puss wandering around in the damp grass and the sky just turning blue to greet the day. Shortly, she would be sitting next to her special friends Kate and Arthur, enjoying breakfast. Later she would go for coffee to Elaine's house where, no doubt, Elaine will have news of Martin the chef and maybe even her son, the elusive Grant.

She was happy to feel appreciated and to live in a safe, caring, and friendly environment. We shall leave Mitsy here, and wish her good health and many more happy and interesting years at Appledore House.

If you enjoyed reading **_What Mitsy Did Next_**, I would be delighted if you would consider writing a short review for me. You can do this on https://www.amazon.co.uk. Reviews are very important for authors, as well as for anyone wondering whether to order a book, so any way in which you can help is much appreciated!

All my books are available via Amazon or to order through any good bookseller. They are also held in the British Library and in some local libraries. They are available in paperback and e-book editions. Further information can be found on the following pages.

You can also checkout my Facebook author page www.facebook.com/carolesusansmith which provides news, updates and information about current activities.

If you would like to send me any comments, feedback or criticism you can message me on the Facebook page as I love to hear from readers!

MEMOIRS BY THIS AUTHOR

TravelWorks

HomeWorks

Oh, and another thing…

NOVELS BY THIS AUTHOR

14 Viney Hill

The Enduring Curiosity of Mitsy Howard: A Walk in the Mill

Mitsy Howard: In the Dark

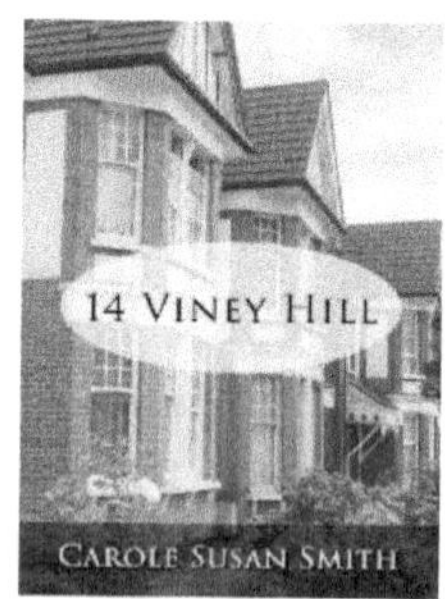